BELIEVING EVERYTHING
An Anthology of New Writing

BELIEVING EVERYTHING
An Anthology of New Writing

Edited by Mary Logue and Lawrence Sutin

Illustrations by Lynn Weaver

Holy Cow! Press · MINNEAPOLIS · 1980

Indexed in <u>SSI 79-83</u>

Acknowledgments: Kate Green's "Abortion Journal" includes previously published material. On page 54, a passage from "The Dead Seal Near McClure's Beach" is reprinted from *The Morning Glory, Prose Poems* by Robert Bly by permission of Harper and Row, Publishers, Inc. © 1975 by Robert Bly. On page 55, a passage from "song for womb fruit" is reprinted from *at the barre* by candyce clayton by permission of Holy Cow! Press © 1978 by candyce clayton. On pages 55 and 57, a line from "August" is reprinted from *Diving Into The Wreck* by Adrienne Rich by permission of W. W. Norton & Co. © 1973 by Adrienne Rich. On page 56, a brief passage from "A Letter to Kate" by Pat Crain is reprinted by permission of the author. And, on page 56, a line from "The Abortion" is reprinted from *All My Pretty Ones* by Anne Sexton by permission of Houghton-Mifflin Company © 1961 by Anne Sexton.

Published by Holy Cow! Press
Post Office Box 618, Minneapolis, Minnesota 55440
Manufactured in the United States of America

Cover illustration and all graphics by Lynn Weaver

Typesetting by John Minczeski of Peregrine Cold Type, St. Paul, Mn

First Printing — Fall, 1980

This project is supported by a grant from the National Endowment for the Arts in Washington, D.C., a federal agency.

Library of Congress Cataloging in Publication Data
Main entry under title:

Believing everything, an anthology of new writing.

    1. American prose literature—20th century.
I. Logue, Mary, 1952— II. Sutin, Lawrence, 1951—
PS659.B38   818'.540808   79-91217
ISBN 0-930100-06-9 (pbk.)

This anthology is dedicated to the memory of:

Helen Patricia Logue
(1954-1979)

CONTENTS

TO THE GENTLE READER

The editors wish to make clear to any and all comers that the stories, journals, flights, yarns, fancies and tales included here under the banner, "Believing Everything" were not chosen with the classic laws of the anthology form in mind. We picked what we liked from the batches the mail brought us. What links the pieces together? As editors we find that quality prevails, highlighted by intensity of voice and subtlety of tone. Please do see for yourself.

Back in the 1930s Henry Miller, Anais Nin, Lawrence Durrell and others in and about depression Paris started a magazine called the "Booster". What those then uneminent folks had to say on the fine art of nudging writers together into a hybrid, pagebound creature still holds true for us:

". . . we are fluid, quixotic, unprincipled. We have no aesthetic canons to preserve or defend. We prefer quality when we can get it, and if we can't have quality then we want what is downright wretched. . . We wish everybody well and no gravel in the kidneys. Signing off. . ."

Mary Logue
Lawrence Sutin

P.S. Lynn Weaver's drawings, more than a complement, are an illumination of the book. Jim Perlman, who leads the Holy Cow to pasture, has guided us to the printer and back with calm, quiet steps.

BELIEVING EVERYTHING
An Anthology of New Writing

Home Cooking

Lynn Lauber

AFTER I'D known him a while, I began staying over at his grand-mother's, Etta's, house. Marlon was by his own admission a street man, and much too energetic to sit still for a good minute with one woman without feeling anxious about missing out on other possibilities, so he left me there, popping beans and rolling Etta's hair, taken care of for all intents and purposes.

That afternoon he fucked me, fast and furtively, on the screened-in porch, worried that she would wander out looking for the newspaper.

"Pull them pants down quick," he said, wiggling on top with a scent of basketball shoes and suede. He kept his head sharply averted away from me so I couldn't even see his eyes and came silently and abruptly. He wiped himself off with a mildewed doily and sauntered casually back into the living room, leaving me stunned and dazed like I'd just been hit by a tornado that I hadn't even seen coming. I sat on the porch for a while, not thinking about anything, my hair in disarray, sperm running lazily down my leg.

"Get dressed, girl," he barked from the living room, not even giving satisfaction a chance to register, had it been there at all. I tried to wander back in nonchalantly, but Etta always knew.

"There's a washrag in the bathroom," she said as Marlon's car pulled out of the driveway.

"Where's he going?" I asked.

"Out running with Eddie and them, I guess," she said.

I washed myself off with a sigh and sat down on the toilet to study Etta's cosmetics. A box of dark umber face powder the consistency of ground cinnamon lay open on the back of the toilet. Southern Rose, the dusty box read, and I looked closely to see the tiny, old fashioned print on the lid: "For an Ebony Sheen Each Time You Preen." Next to it were a variety of blunt eyebrow pencils that Etta used to blacken her heavy brows and the tiny grey roots at the front of her hair. A tin of Black and White Ointment that smelled sweetly of wild roses also lay open, a few curly hairs trapped beneath the thick, pale grease. Once when I had mistakenly used her brush my hair had been gluey and lank with the stuff all night, stuck to my head like it had been painted on.

"You gotta remember, honey," she had laughed looking at me. "There are some differences."

Then we wiled away the evening, swinging on the back porch, baking sweet potato pies, waiting for the men to come back home. Slim, Marlon's father, lived there, too, and only came back late at night when he ate and fell immediately into a stupor from trying to service too many women for too many years. Etta, it seemed, had sons everywhere: big, dark faceless men with names like Lamont and Little Otis, who lived in Detroit and California. I knew little about any of them, except the color of their two-tone Cadillacs, the year of their Monte Carlos, and that they often had white girlfriends.

"This here is Lamont's girl," Etta said, handing me a picture of a dazed looking blonde in a short pink skirt. "She works in a shoe factory in Sacramento."

I looked at the picture closely and then handed it back.

"You surprised at all us white girls?" I asked, seriously, because she never acted like it, never treated me any way except like old time family.

"You forget how old I am, darlin'," she said. And she was right. I did.

I spent the rest of the evening laying on Marlon's bed leafing through the sepia photos in Etta's old picture albums. She looked the same, back then in the 30's, only better. Gangly and lean she posed against gleaming DeSotos with rough looking men in turned down caps.

"Who's this?" I asked.

"Aw," she said grinning. "That was Royce. He was a number's runner in St. Louis and was in love with me like you wouldn't believe." She stopped and smiled hard, seriously. "Loved me to death."

"Why didn't you marry him?" I asked.

She looked up at me with surprise and, for the first time I could remember, like I was really young and green.

"Girl, you can't hardly marry everyone who loves you," she said.

And then seeing my blank look, she laughed, a deep resounding gale of tumbling sound, and put her arms around me until she was finished, which seemed like a very long time.

It was almost dawn before Marlon got in that night and I feigned sleep as he stripped and climbed into bed, reeking of a junglely scent that I knew was a mixture of whiskey, cologne and other women's arms. He pulled the stained chenile bedspread tight around his neck and grabbed my thigh, feeling around for an opening.

"Kiss me," I said sleepily when he scooted on top, but he just ignored it. He buried his head in the pillow next to us and worked diligently away while I lay quietly inert holding his hand, trying to conjure up real romance. Soon he was snoring loudly, his mouth open like a donkey, and I thought, "I should be content. I have a man beside me and I'm in a warm bed." But then Etta's mattress creaked wearily above me and I heard her sigh so deeply and entirely that I dropped his hand and sighed too, letting our poor discontent mingle into a tired, old wind that curled out and up into the alleyways.

It was early spring so when I woke the smell of new grass was in the air along with the aroma of Etta's bacon that she fried, thick and hand cut, each morning. She made runny eggs and strong black coffee and we played B. B. King and sat in the sun, waiting for time to wake us up.

"Why don't you get you a new dress and we'll go out tonight," Marlon said, in a good mood for him.

"Can we really?" I asked.

"Yeh, yeh, do you hair up nice and we'll go," he said abruptly, catching himself at being a bit too nice and rising from the table.

Etta winked at me, got up too, and went over and pinched him on the ass.

"Being nice like that ain't exactly going to kill you," she said.

He went silently into the bathroom and urinated loudly. He never talked back to Etta, though he would've beaten up anybody else in a minute for saying much less. He left the house without another word and she stood at the window watching as he pulled out of the driveway.

"Grandson or not, I sure hate to see you feeling grateful for little bits of kindness like that," she said. "You might get to thinking that's all you deserve and never ask for nothing better."

She turned and studied me closely.

"How old are you anyhow?"

"Seventeen," I lied.

She looked back out the window though I knew there was nothing there anymore.

"That's too young," she said, mostly to herself. "Too young to only expect that."

I sat out on the porch that night, my hair teased in a wild, tangled ball and watched the street lights go up and the sun go down before Etta finally came out to get me.

"Come on in," she said. "He ain't coming."

I avoided her eyes as I went into the bathroom and wiped off the thick pink makeup that had coalesced into oil with the heat. Though I felt tired and dejected, I sat up with her to watch Lawrence Welk, eating the popcorn she served in an old tuliped bowl while she clucked and moaned at the dancing on TV.

"Move them feet," she shouted at the screen. "Loosen up," but I knew she was just trying to distract me.

Slim sauntered in finally, long and grinny, with a flashy ebony woman situated on his arm like a pet bird. She jingled into the room with her brassy jewelry and instantly filled it with a dense, fruity scent like overripe peaches. Etta nodded at her as she nestled down with Slim on the couch, but seemed annoyed at her presence and began dusting the end tables and vacuuming around so that the TV was obliterated.

"Quiet, mama," Slim kept yelling, until it was clear that she either couldn't hear him or had decided to pretend she couldn't.

The woman sat back and studied Etta with detachment as she ran her thin, brown hands up and down the shiny material of Slim's thighs. She glanced at me very briefly, the way you look at a lamp or a bookend, and I saw that up close her face was sagged, collapsed, like cement when it hasn't set completely.

When Slim left the room she turned and looked at me again.

"You one of Marlon's?" she asked.

"Yes," I said quietly. "I'm his girlfriend."

"Oh." She arched an eyebrow and laughed abruptly, situating her arm around the back of the couch like a long coiled snake.

"His girlfriend, huh?" she said, looking at me closely. "Old Marlon's getting fancy on us, ain't he?"

I smiled weakly and watched the woman on TV twirl frantically around, waltzing contently in the same useless circle, but I felt her gaze steady on my cheek.

"If you is girlfriend why ain't he here?"

I felt sweaty and weak and looked helplessly at Etta who veered the vacuum intently into the hall, her mouth set and hard.

"He's got other things to do, I guess," I said.

"Looks like you ain't satisfying him, honey," she said, moving closer and curving her mouth in a wide, angled grin. "Bet that surprises you. Guess you thought you'd be keeping him home with that fine white tail."

She chuckled low, deep down in her throat, but when I looked over again her smile had turned, twisted into a hard metallic slash and she wasn't staring at me at all, her gaze tilted at a spot near the corner, a place somewhere near my shoes.

"Guess that's what all ya'll think," she said flatly. "And it aint't even yours to be thinking about."

Etta continued vacuuming until she ran out of space, straightened a few doilies, and then motioned for me to follow as she climbed the steps to her room.

"You're sleeping up here tonight," she said as we reached the top. "I don't want you down there around all that."

I laid down in the space she made beside her and stared at her large bony feet sticking out of the quilt.

"Who is she?" I asked.

"A whore," Etta said. "Her name's Hilda and she's been with every man in town and their daddies, too."

She turned over on her side and spoke to the peeling wall.

"She just messes with Slim because he spends money like a fool. Mine, if you want to know the truth."

I turned off the light and closed my eyes, feeling her warmth being absorbed into the sheets, the air.

"Why's her face like that?" I asked after awhile.

Etta rolled back over on her back and we both clicked open our eyes again and stared at the same darkness, the same black yawn.

"Because men treated her bad for years," she said finally, moving her foot under my heel so it touched just lightly, like a brace, a bolster, a gentle cushion.

After that night Marlon was gone most all the time, having fallen in love with a variety of new women, including a herd of black studies students who were home for the summer.

"I've gotta start taking pride in my race," he said one night as he got into bed with me begrudgingly. "I can't be running around with no white girls."

"We don't run around," I said meekly. "We never even leave the house."

He yanked the covers off of me and turned his brown, bumpy back to my face.

"Don't argue with me," he said. "I'm just sick of your ass in my bed every night. Go on home."

I sat up in the middle of the bed, rubbing my knees, afraid to touch him.

"Come on, Marlon," I pleaded. "Nobody needs to know about us."

But he could become a piece of wood when he wanted and though I cajoled, cuddled and dripped tears smack in his face, he wouldn't talk anymore. I padded into the bathroom and sat on the toilet eating a chicken leg, looking at my pale, pinched face in the mirror. After a long while Etta came to the door and stood looking in at me, her hair in rags, her face oiled like an iron skillet.

"What'd he do?" she asked evenly.

"He wants me to leave."

She studied me for awhile, her hands on her hips, and then turned back into the kitchen.

"You're not going nowhere," she said. "I'll take care of him."

And in her own way, I guess she did, the best that anyone could take care of Marlon. Though there were never any lapses into anything resembling real kindness, he wasn't actually mean to me either. He simply avoided coming home almost entirely, leaving just Etta and me to press his shiny, two piece suits and bake pies that nobody ate.

Women with low, syrupy voices began calling late at night, insisting on knowing where he was.

"I don't know, really," I'd say, my stomach tight and sad, but then Etta would grab the phone seeing my stricken face.

"Don't be calling here asking no questions," she'd tell them. "He'd be with you if he wanted you to know."

During the day I began going through his pockets and drawers, looking for even more evidence. I found bundles of perfumed love letters, many from months before, written on pastel stationery in a feminine, curly script.

"I thank God for our night together and you," one said, among other things.

I sat in the middle of Marlon's bed and wondered how he acted with her, whoever she was, and why she thanked God for it.

"It's just gonna make you feel worse rooting through all that," Etta said, watching me read. "Seems to me you do enough of that already."

I folded up the letters and looked at our reflection in the dresser mirror, Etta solemnly folding clothes, me sitting pale and useless in the middle of the bed.

"Maybe he just won't ever be good to me," I said finally.

Etta put down the socks she was matching and looked up at me in the mirror, a mixture of sadness and relief passing over her face.

"Sugar," she said simply, "I been waiting for you to wonder about that," and went to her room for the rest of the day.

Tape Subject: Groupwork

Thomas Zigal

Side A

Test, one, two. *Pop. Pop.* I suppose you're on. . . . Shelley's gone
up to bed, Peter for a walk. Tonight's session was particularly
heavy, and to tell the truth, I'm still a little freaked out myself. I
knew Margot was an epileptic, but I didn't really think we were
pushing her too hard. We were just trying to get her to stop
playing dumb, that's all. Shelley brought up her nervousness
around men—how Margot always relates to them as the helpless,
ignorant female. She began to escalate like crazy, screaming at
Shelley that she'd betrayed a confidence, or something—I don't
know. She'd been crying for quite a while when Peter tried to
put his arms around her. That seemed to trigger it. . . . I thought
the ambulance would never get here. She bit all the way through
my wallet. . . . Man, it's amazing what'll come down when you're
not willing to dump out all your anxieties. . . .
The group discussed it after she was taken away. Our agitation
was pretty evident—we were pretty strung out—but after awhile
everyone seemed to settle down and cope—except maybe Peter,
who was stony silent and then left for a walk. . . . Shelley told
them that in a roundabout sort of way we'd done Margot a favor.
Mr. and Mrs. Riley expressed doubt, and if I hadn't come to
Shelley's defense, she may've lost their confidence. Sometimes I
worry about her development as a counselor.

Having Peter as a housemate has its advantages. Whenever I
feel he's walling himself off or experiencing some kind of
hostility, I can easily get him down in the Group Room and work
it out. I knew he was uptight about last night, so I spread the
crayolas and construction paper on the floor and asked him to
get in touch with his primal feelings—his Kid. . . . He tacked up
his latest contract on the back of the door, next to the others'. I
can read the large crayon print from here: *Peter will show his*

19

emotions. He will cry when he needs to. He will not be afraid to ask for loving strokes when he wants them. He will open up. He will stop rationalizing everything. He will admit when he is wrong or when he has failed . . . Uh, oh, the phone's ringing. Be back in a minute. . . . It was Sharon over at the Group House. She says she has a difficult client, some twenty-year-old named Angela who needs re-siring badly. She wants us to take her on because of our luck with live-ins. I told her I'd have to discuss it with Shelley and Peter, but they're usually easy to convince. If they agree, we can use the next group session for the girl's initiation.

I guess I shouldn't be surprised that Angela's re-siring initiation completely unglued the Rileys. They're a middle-aged couple, a different generation and all that, and so far they've been real obstructions to the group's growth. I'm glad they split, but their request for partial reimbursement of their money presents a problem. We haggled over it—a bad scene, completely tacky— and I couldn't convince them that a contract's a contract—all or nothing. They'll get their lawyer; I'll get mine. . . . Oh, well. . . . The rest of the group had no problem. Even Peter seemed more relaxed, involved. I watched him during the ceremony, his eyes searching all over Angela wrapped up in the cotton blanket on the floor . . . puffing his pipe like a wise old professor, *(laughs)* shaking that little baby rattler to coo her. Really a trip!
I let Shelley handle most of the initiation; she needs to assert herself more if she's gonna make it in this profession. She didn't seem to have any trouble, though . . . fed Angela from the bottle like her own mother. I was a little concerned when we unraveled the blanket and had to get down to business, but Shelley took the scissors and carefully snipped away at the girl's pubic hair like a surgeon at work, until only a dark stubble remained there. The Rileys showed embarrassment and confusion—quick, surprised glances . . . whispering—and I knew we'd finally pushed their buttons. I couldn't tell if it was the nudity or the ceremonial shearing that undid them. They were on their way to the door before we even brought out the baby powder.

When I returned from the hassle in the driveway, the other
members were sprinkling Angela's stomach and thighs with
powder, smoothing it across her glossy skin till she was chalky as
a corpse. She took it well . . . eyes closed, goo-gooing like a baby,
her lean legs rocking back and forth. Shelley told them
something like 'Vincent and I are her new parents. We'll let her
grow up at her own pace.' That's the right idea, anyway. For a
change, I felt no need to correct her information.

I was tempted to come down last night, right after our
confrontation, and record my feelings; but I'm afraid she
would've taken my leaving the bed as more rejection. I guess I
should've been more diplomatic, but there's *no way* my body can
handle her on top, man. We tried it before, after she'd lost
thirty-five pounds, and I still couldn't bear the weight. Naturally
all this brought up the whole obesity thing again—she accused
me of insensitivity and frigidity. I lost my cool and told her she
was nothing but a mixed-up, adolescent cow when she first came
to group therapy, and I'd not only gotten her to be more self-
aware, I'd supported her all the way down to 200 pounds and
even bought her some makeup and a few nice dresses that
complimented her shape. 'Big deal!' she said, 'that's only because
you wanted to hump me like all the other chicks in the group.'
Man, that hacked me off. I rolled out of bed and lit a cigar. I was
furious! 'And that's why I asked you to marry me?' I said. 'That's
why I sent you through counselors' training?' She began to
whimper and whine like she always does. 'Then why won't you
let me get on top?' Thank god Angela started crying in her
bedroom. Shelley threw on her robe and shuffled out of the room
to fix the bottle. . . . It took me off the hook. I didn't have to
tell her I thought she was gaining weight again.

Another session over. . . . I feel high. The energy level tonight
was super! Margot was back, a little pale and quiet, but as soon
as we went upstairs to bathe Angela she seemed to perk up a
little. Everyone did, especially Peter, who has a *thing* for our

little babe, I'm sure. You can't blame him, though; the girl's very
pretty . . . soft brown eyes, kinky dark hair coiled to her
shoulders. And when I see her naked, like this evening, I
certainly can't control my own turn-on. (*laughs*) I just hope
Shelley didn't notice the bulge in my pants, or it's liable to be
one more stamp against me in her collection.
As for Angela, she's progressing well. Children aren't my
modality, but if I were to guess, I'd say she's three or four now.
She talks in complete sentences, though simple and girlish. I
could tell she enjoyed all the attention we were giving her in the
tub. At one point Peter knelt down to rescue a sinking toy
animal, and she blew a drift of bubbles into his face. Hah! Even
he found it funny. I think he's finally beginning to lighten up
some.

I can't believe last night was so together and this morning
everything's hyper tense. It all started so innocently with me
taking out the garbage, of all things. . . . I found an empty
chocolates box at the bottom of the can—one of those Sampler
deals. I brought it back inside and placed it in front of Shelley at
the breakfast table without saying a word. At first she denied it
was hers . . . even claimed she'd seen Peter buy it. I smoked my
cigar and smiled . . . smiled and smoked . . . completely silent,
listening to her weak defenses. Finally she began to pound the
table, rattling our cups and saucers. She said I'd grown distant,
and my coldness had caused her to break her diet . . . that she
was a victim of societal programming, mistrusted all her life by
authority figures, etcetera. 'Yeah, I've gained ten goddamn
pounds in the last fuckin' week!' she screamed at me.
I tried to remain calm and speak softly. I told her she was
inventing a bunch o' garbage and, naturally, projecting shit on
me—her own guilt trips. She didn't let me finish, and neither did
Peter, because by then she was yelling and he was downstairs and
in some sort of rage himself—about his room. He said that
someone had *violated his privacy*, to use his words.
Shelley and I followed him up to his room. . . . The cat was still
in the closet, clawing its way up the sleeve of Peter's nice suede

dinner jacket. His shirts and sweaters were wadded up on the
racks, snagged in places . . . some were piled on the floor like
rags. There was a nauseous stink over everything.
Peter refused to touch it, so I had to remove the frightened little
thing, its claws clinging like barbs to the fabric. 'It's probably
been in my closet all night!' he said, nearly hysterical. 'And I'm
sure it didn't wander in there all by itself!'
I took one look at the closet floor and realized he was right.
There were chunks of crayon mashed into the wood under the
heap of clothing. 'Oh, shit,' Shelley said. 'Little Angela's been up
to her tricks again.'
Peter let out his anger and frustration for several minutes, pacing
the floor like a madman. He demanded repayment for damaged
clothes, and he wanted someone to scrub the red and purple
marks off the floor. I said I would have a talk with Angela
immediately.
'No you won't,' Shelley said, as spiteful as I've ever seen her. 'I'll
talk to her myself. She responds to *me*. *You* obviously don't
understand how to deal with the female sex.' I asked her what all
of a sudden gave her such illuminating insight into human
behavior, but she stormed away without another word, leaving
me with an irate and restless Peter.

Things are getting a bit strange around here. . . . I don't know
quite what to make of it yet. . . . Peter called me today from his
office and asked me to meet him for lunch. He said it was
terribly important—and secret—and not to mention it to anyone.
Well, as soon as I sat down with him over at La Boheme I could
tell he was upset. He wasn't eating, just knocking down cup after
cup of coffee and speeding like an addict. I asked him what was
wrong, and he told me he thought he ought to move out.
'Whatever for?' I asked, and he began to relate what went on in
his room last night.
It seems that he'd just crawled into bed when someone knocked
gently on his door. Our little Angela traipsed in, dressed in what
we've now determined were Shelley's clothes—the dress
swallowed her like a sack and dragged along the carpet . . . her
high-heel shoes flip-flopped noisily . . . a Sunday hat was stuck

haphazardly on her head. Around her neck was a string of pearls, and her wrists jingled from too much jewelry. Peter switched on his bedside lamp and could see she'd been into Shelley's rouge and lipstick, and had sloppily lined her already-dark eyebrows with pencil. She'd even attempted false eyelashes, but one sagged noticeably. He said she sat on the edge of the bed and removed a compact from the purse looped around her arm. She stared into the tiny mirror and powdered her face like the *femme fatale* in some thirties movie.

When Peter asked her what she wanted, she apparently started talking in a little girl's voice about playing dolls with him. At this point in the story, Peter became extremely embarrassed and hummed and hawed, downing his coffee quickly. He lit his pipe with an uneasy hand. . . . It seems he was overcome by the situation—'she seemed so *innocent* and all,' he said—so he went along with her, and eventually they were playing Doctor and Nurse, and eventually he'd stripped her down—dress and hat and gobs of jewelry—and they were going at it hot and heavy for the next hour or so. She smeared rouge and mascara all over him and his sheets. I must admit, the incident sounds *incredibly* sensuous.

But Peter was totally wrecked by it . . . he considered himself a child molester (*laughs*). I had to remind him that in all reality Angela is a twenty-year-old woman, with twenty-year-old hormones, and she's fully capable of handling her own sexuality. 'Wait a minute,' he said, 'either she's twenty years old or she's a re-siring eleven-year-old, but you can't have it both ways. Otherwise the whole process is pointless.' I couldn't argue with that, so I told him to avoid her in the future . . . just stay out of her way, and lock his door at night. I promised to discuss it with Shelley and see what could be done.

Shelley's being a bitch. I told her about the incident and she pretended not to believe Peter. 'He's a totally hung-up dude,' she said. 'He's into sexual fantasies—you know that. It's all he ever talks about in group . . . he's scripted to see women as unattainable sex objects. Not gettin' any for months has finally gone to his head.' She said she doubted if Angela had even been

to his room last night. I asked her if we could sit Angela down
and ask her about it, but she got huffy again and said the girl
was too young to be corrupted by Peter's filthy fantasies. She
refused to bring it up with her *little darling*, as she put it. . . . I
may have to take things into my own hands.

Click. Pop, pop, pop. Hi, Daddy Vincent. You didn't expect
anybody to find your little tape, did you? (*giggles*) How silly!
You shoulda been more careful—I mean, right on your study
recorder, in plain sight? (*giggles*) Boy, could I tell Mother a thing
or two. But I won't, honest I won't, if you promise to take me
rollerskating . . . or something more exciting, maybe. (*giggles*)
You crazy ol' boob, you. . . . Bye, now. . . . *Click.*

Side B

Wow, am I fagged out! I thought the session this evening would
never end . . . . It was the first time in my five-years' experience
as a counselor that I nearly lost control of the group—and
Shelley is the one who started it all. I can't believe she'd do a
thing like that . . . after all I've been through with her . . . It
amounted to sabotage! She was trying to get Father Johns to
laugh, and he was being his usual tight-assed self, so she began
to tickle him. All I said was I thought tickling too coercive—that
he ought to laugh naturally or not at all—and she turned on me
like a mental case, her mood switching 180 degrees, and I
realized that she was about to cash in all the stamps she'd been
collecting against me for a long time.
Anyway, she called me a *fascist* and an *authoritarian pig* and a
few other names I can't recall. To my surprise Margot and Jim
jumped in, and soon I was made out to be some kind of cigar-
smoking despot. But I encouraged 'em to get it out; I even baited
'em. When Peter and Father Johns came to my defense, I asked
them to stay out of it. Shelley and the others needed to vent
their anger. What I didn't expect was for them to start throwing
things. Thank god it was only the cushions. What if there were
glass objects in the room? Or if we'd taken our coffee break

already and mugs were lying around? I wouldn't be talking into
this microphone right now, that's for damn sure.

More crap today . . . this time from Angela. I went into the
kitchen for a sandwich and discovered a sink full of dirty
dishes—and after I'd *expressly* told her to do them this morning,
along with her other chores. I found her stretched out on the
couch, slouching around in the jeans and tee-shirt she's been
wearing for two days, reading some trashy movie magazine with
Robert Redford and Barbara Streisand on the cover. A Coke can
and candy wrappers were strewn all around on the carpet.
'I thought I told you to do the dishes,' I said. She never looked up
from her magazine, just sing-songed she *didn't have to* 'cause her
Mom didn't tell her to. She made it clear she only took orders
from Shelley.
I became annoyed—spoke harsher than I intended. 'Don't you
dare talk that way to your father,' I said. 'Now you get in there
and do those dishes!' She didn't say a word . . . turned a page . . .
acted like I wasn't there. I don't know what's under my skin
lately—I really lost it: 'You're not too big for me to turn over my
knee and give a good swatting to, young lady!' I said. She let the
magazine fall across her chest and gave me a look I won't forget
for a long time . . . a cold, mature, mischievous stare, not a
teenager's impudence, but the calculating smirk of a grown
woman: 'You'd like that, wouldn't you,' she said.
It unnerved me, I'll admit quite frankly. I played dumb . . . I, I
said something about not liking it at all but doing it as a duty if
she didn't behave, or some such rot. She laughed. 'Peter likes it
too,' she said. 'Likes what?' I asked. 'To spank me.'
Well, I couldn't believe it; I chalked it up to pubescent fantasy.
She insisted, though, that on two occasions Peter had spanked
her for being a *bad girl*, once in her room, once in his. 'In my
panties,' she giggled.
To me it didn't matter if it was true or not. I knew she would be
gone in another week or so but that Peter would have to live on
with us—and with himself. I asked her to leave him alone. 'Tell
it to *him*,' she said. 'He's the one that's doin' it.'

I told her Sharon and I had to go out of town tomorrow morning to conduct a group retreat up in Santa Rosa, and that when I got back I wanted the house as clean as a battleship. I also said to avoid Peter. She picked up the magazine again and started reading. . . . Jesus, I never had this much conflict with our live-ins before.

Well, I don't know quite what to say or how to say it . . . I feel completely spaced out . . . very hyper. The minute I got back from Santa Rosa things were strained. I could tell that right away because Shelley and Angela were sunbathing in the back yard and paid no attention to me at all when I greeted them. Shelley lifted her face, pushed back her sunglasses, and said *Oh, hi,* as if I hadn't been away for two days. . . . Then I found Peter's note in my desk drawer, and everything since has been a bad dream. . . . I called the accounting office immediately but they said he'd phoned in sick and wouldn't be back for a few days. They had no idea he'd moved and couldn't tell me his new address. I checked his room, and sure enough he'd taken everything but the furniture. His drawers were empty except for a paperclip or two. A lone hanger lay on the closet floor near the crayon marks. . . . Poor guy. If what he said in the letter was true, I had to be extremely tactful in the way I handled things. Obviously I couldn't lose my head and attack Shelley and Angela outright. . . . Rope burns on his wrists and ankles, his chest and phallic hair shaved clean. God, it's hard to believe they'd do a thing like that! He said they were stoned out of their minds, so I don't know. . . . He even went along with it for awhile, he said . . . laughed along with them . . . thought foolishly, when they took his clothes off and started playing with him, that they had *other* intentions. I guess everything just got carried away. . . . Poor strung-out fella—always needing attention. He really got it this time. I lit a cigar and went down to the back yard where they lay side by side like two companions at the beach, Shelley's pale folds of flesh taking on a stark obscenity in the plainness of day. Angela had her top down but I refused to stare. I told them I called Peter's office just to say I was back, and they'd informed me of

his call-in. When I checked his room I found it vacant. 'What's going on?' I asked, acting as naive as I could.
Shelley said they'd had a fight and he'd finally realized he no longer fit in the household. When I pressed her about what'd started it, she said she and Angela were in our bedroom watching t.v. and Peter kept barging in, bothering them—he wanted to watch it too, but they didn't want his company, or something like that—and one thing led to another . . . an exchange of words . . . name-calling, etcetera. 'We finally just blew up at each other and got everything we'd wanted to say for months off our chests,' she said. 'The guy's a real dork. We don't need him around here anymore.' The story appeared respectable—but it differed widely from Peter's version, of course. He maintained he caught them naked together on our waterbed, the room reeking with marijuana smoke, the t.v. set blaring full blast. He tried not to act shocked, he said, but he must've been obvious in his disapproval 'cause they went after him, *unabashedly nude*, as he put it, and enticed him back into the room. . . . Could that really've been the way it happened? I don't know. At this point I'm totally confused.

Pop. Am I on? *Pop, pop.* Okay. . . . Don't worry, Vincent dear, I'm gonna clear everything up for ya. Angela told me about your little tape *memoirs (laughs)*, so I decided to check it out for myself. I'm glad I did. Now I'm completely convinced that you're a liar and an asshole—just like Peter, in fact. For the record, sweetheart, we didn't do anything to the little prick he didn't ask for—and that's a fact. He really got off to it. The reason he packed up and split, I'm sure, is because he was afraid you'd find out and come down hard on him like you always do. . . . Man, and to think I've put up with you this long! Well, it's clear to me now that you're in deep trouble, babe—you can't distinguish what's really happenin' from your little psych masturbations here, which are at best a bunch of half-truths colored by your own distorted perceptions . . . your whole Big Daddy ego number, ya know. So as of today I'm taking over the group

sessions. And the very first thing I'm gonna suggest, Vincent
darling, is that we re-sire *you*. Yes, you heard it right! From
cradle on up . . . which, by the way, is how we got started with
Peter the other night—the shaving and all. I guess we were too
fucked up to realize it was the wrong place and time, (*laughs*)
and the wrong guy. Oh, and another thing before I go. Angela is
her normal age again—fairly well adjusted, considering *your*
influence—and she's gonna stay on with us. . . . We like each
other fine. . . . At least she lets me get on top once in awhile.

I've been crying; I admit it. (*clears throat*) It's something I rarely
do—once a year, maybe. But after all the screaming and yelling it
seemed natural, like the only thing left to do. . . . I don't usually
wind back the tape and listen to it, but for some reason I did this
evening—call it intuition, I guess—and I discovered Shelley's
raving monologue, so I searched back farther and found a short
message from Angela—a cute little ditty from a more innocent
period in her growth. . . . What can I say? I went right for their
throats, so to speak, no holds barred, (*clears throat*) not even the
pretense of being constructive. . . . 'Let's get it all out front,' I
said. So we did. . . . Hell, what an evening! They're up there in
my bedroom—*their* bedroom now, so they tell me—sleeping like
innocent babes, like nothing happened at all. . . . *I* can't sleep . . .
I don't feel human any more, to tell the truth. I feel gutted and
hung out to rot like an animal carcass. . . . And I'm tired—man,
am I tired, and sick of all this! My head's buzzing. I'd just like to
see it end peacefully, in some kind of honorable compromise,
where none of the parties are hurt too badly. But not Shelley!
She's out for blood, damn her. . . . Maybe I'll go for a long walk
and try to clear my head. I've gotta figure out some way to stay
on top of all this.

Me again. . . . I'm surprised I've never hung out much in here
before—it was always *his* study. But I'm actually startin' to get
off to this whole tape biz. It's kind o' like being a kid again and
sneaking through your ol' man's drawers . . . sort of a rush, like.
Anyway, Vincent won't be needing this room, not for many

moons; so I thought, I mean, after all, if the recorder's here you may as well play with it. Right?

I can't believe it was so smooth dealin' with him. I mean, last night he was flippin' out and runnin' around like a hurt little twit; this morning he's snoozing away in Peter's room, a little darling wrapped up in a cotton blanket. Angela's up there with the bottle right now. She's into a mother trip now, and it fits her okay.

When we came downstairs early this morning we found him curled up on the living room carpet, an ashtray piled up with cigar butts at his side, ashes all over him like some kind o' derelict or somethin'. The room stank like a pool hall. . . . I shook him; he wouldn't budge. I shook him harder and he started moanin'. He opened his eyes and didn't seem to snap to who I was at first, then he started crying and babbling like a fool. I looked at Angela, and she had it down what to do—osmosis, I guess—you just pick these things up after a while. . . . We knew there wasn't time to call the whole group together. We figured they'd understand once we explained what kind of heavy emergency was goin' down. . . . So she immediately went for the scissors. Freaky about Vincent, though. Like I still can't get over it. Angie and I were ready to jump on his case today—we'd rapped through some stragedies—but he folded like an accordian. *Nolo Contendere*. I swear, there was even this big ol' weird smile on his face the whole time we were rubbing him down with the baby oil.

(*whispers*) Shelley, hon, my sweet little sow, my juicy hunk o' horsemeat. You've got a lot to learn about strategies. Did you forget who you were dealing with? Gah-gah, goo-goo, and all that, my dear. (*laughs*) Baby Vincent has been suckling his mother Angela for hours now—and twice he managed to crawl back in her womb. (*laughs*) Oh, I wouldn't try to tear her away from her little darling if I were you, either. She's quite attached. *Click.*

The czar contemplates
the Garden of Erotica

Regina de Cormier-Shekerjian

The Czar contemplates the Garden of Erotica
and finds it wanting roses. But he is not
surprised for after all has he not always
known that Mary lives in a small the smallest
room at the top of the palace behind closed
doors surrounded by three armed guards and the
wolves of great hunger rendering her virtually
inaccessible? He agrees thus to write his
memoirs yes and a history of imagined future
triumphs but dozes off after tea and too much
black currant jam dreaming of the garden he
had left in haste despair left without making
provisions for the coming winter the one
hundred and fifty one days of frozen desire the
samovar hissing petulantly away in the long
dark afternoons the biscuits crumbling in the
dry mouth the old mouth of wanting the wolves
whining on the landing and he stumbling now
back down the stairs out into the perfumed
garden promising the young the very young new
maidservant five kopeks for silence and her
services as guide to Our Unknown Lady of the
Tongues Yet to be Deciphered. When he is
awakened at six he catches a glimpse of himself in the czarina's gilded Rococo mirror
and boxes the ears of the maidservant vowing
to throw her and the rest of the household to
the bears in the forest. Later that evening
he asks for a second helping of meat and drinks
more than his share of the vintage wine that
had been laid down for a different occasion

noting that the czarina's neck is not as white
not as long not as supple as the maidservant's
and her body he knows for a fact has forgotten
how to sing. Across the table the czarina
in the still-glittering candlelight observes that
the czar must see his physician as soon as
possible about those untimely warts carousing all
over his once splendid body and oh yes she has
engaged a young man from Petersburg to teach her
Greek so that she too might read the literature
of classical love that pure love he her husband
so often speaks of although she had always
thought mistakenly of course that he had been
referring to the troubadours' songs of Saint
Mary not to those of Sappho. That night slipping
into sleep the czar fondles the ruby on his right
little finger and resolves that come spring he will
invade Turkey.

The Lover

Terry Kennedy

I WANT A LOVER so badly I can taste him she told the old crone who inhabited her body and lapped up everything she said as though it were ambrosia. Tecla Jurkelewicz knew that she could no longer go on pantomiming the motions of living. She needed a man.

There had been a green-eyed journalist in the corridor of her memory who refused to let go of her arms even now. She had met him decades ago when she was a young, white-toothed clairol ad of a reporter. Men looked at her then.

He had squeezed tight against her one workday when they were crammed into a conventioneer's elevator on their way to cover the same story. His belt buckle pressed into her backbone as a dozen more men forced themselves on at the 6th floor. She felt a wave of excitement unzip her shyness. "Hello," she said, turning around and smiling at the stranger.

His stare fell onto her lips like a kiss. "My name's Ferdinand Tannenbaum," he winked. She despised his name! How could a creature so gorgeously proportioned, so meticulously groomed, and so outrageously exotic have such an impossible by line?

"What paper are you with?"

She was trying to act detatched. Trying to ignore the erection she knew was pumping up his tight slacks. What the hell kind of a man is this, she thought.

"The Washington Chronicle."

The doors of the elevator burst open just then and the herd of hardware store managers exited. Like inner city boy scouts on their way to the seashore for the first time, they pushed past Tecla unlocking her body from the chemistry of Ferdinand.

"Oh, I used to send them freelance articles for years. Did you ever see my name? Tecla Jurkelewicz. Guess you'd remember a mouthful like that."

She laughed but the crone inside her was livid.

41

"Why did you say anything so asinine? He'll think you're the fool that you are!"

This many years later while Tecla dusted the dining room table and felt hunger moaning behind her flab she still could picture Ferdinand. His blue button-down collar brushing against his neck was as clear as the narcissus plant blooming on her window sill.

"I want a lover."

It was a phrase that had been with her like the lyrics of a grammer school jumping rope chant. Everyday of her life nearly, for close to 41 years it had skipped through her brain since she had met Ferdinand.

Tecla was born in Poland and had come over to this country on a D.P. boat. She had lived in Newark with her aunt Dzidka and had married Michael right after graduation from the tiny Catholic high school on Saint Sebastian Street. She'd never felt dizzy talking to a man until the day she spoke to Ferdinand Tannenbaum.

But that was ridiculously long ago. Now she was nearing her 70th birthday. Thinking such thoughts only filled her with despair over her lack of courage when she was younger. Why didn't she risk taking a lover then? "Taking a lover requires guts," the old crone was screaming.

"You were always chicken."

"Damn you, I wasn't. Didn't I learn the language of this country? Didn't I become a reporter when there was no such thing as woman's lib? Didn't I?"

The crone turned away. She knew Tecla was very brave about some things. It was only when it came to love that she was about as daring as a child trying to ride a two wheeler for the first time.

Tecla kept the polishing cloth moving across the mahogany. In the mirror sheen she saw back into the past. She and Ferdinand got off the elevator on the 16th floor. He asked her if she wanted to go and have a hamburger with him.

"Oh, no. I can't. I mean, well. You see, I'm ah. . . . I'm married. I have three kids. I have. . ."

Suddenly he leaned back against the wall and thrust himself forward in such a way from the waist down, that Tecla blushed. She had never seen a man flirt this way before. He grinned.

"So what's a hamburger? I'm not asking you to go to bed with me."

The telephone rang interrupting Tecla's waxing. She shlepped into the den slowly. Who could be calling her on a Saturday morning before 9? Maybe Michael's car had broken down on his way to the boat. Fishing was all that man ever thought about. Fishing and food.

"Damn glutton."

She picked up the receiver as if it were covered with poison ivy.

"Yah?"

"Ma'am, this is the operator. We have a person to person call for Missus Tekala Jurk leff itch. Is this she?"

"Yah, I'm her."

"Hello, Tecla? This is a friend of yours."

The rug and the floor fell out from under Tecla's sturdy black shoes. Her whole body pulsed like a frightened animal's. After 41 years the voice was exactly the same. "Magnificent," said the crone.

"Ferdinand, how are you?"

"I'm old. So very old."

He was laughing and the crone could see that his hands were covered with sweat.

"I'm a grandfather now. And do you know, Tecla Jurkelewicz, that every night since the day I met you I crawl into my bed and wonder why we never slept together. I had never met a woman who had the effect on me that you did. And, Tecla, never another one since either. We were stupid."

"Ah, yes. Stupid and moral and reporters. I thought it was so unnecessary. I thought a spiritual relationship was all we needed. I thought my husband would die of shame if he found out. I thought my children. . . ."

"Hush, Tecla, that was centuries ago. I'm calling you today because I want you. Do you want to hear about a foolish old man with memories? When I take off my glasses and put them on the nightstand your face is the face that this foolish old man sees. Your lips are the lips I kiss when I say good night to my wife. Your body is the body I press into. Not her's. Oh, Tecla, Tecla! I imagine too much. I am too lonely to be proud. I am begging you to see me. I'm going to Boston next Tuesday, meet me!"

"I will be there."

The sound of her own voice convinced Tecla that she would be.

Calmly she took the name and address of the hotel. Then without so much as a goodbye she hung up. She put away the dust cloth and the furniture cream. She walked up the twenty-one carpeted stairs to her bedroom. She sat on her bed.

She thought of the headboard, the springs, the slats running between the sides. It was a fine bed. A bed she had slept in beside the father of her children for over half a century. But a bed has no heart.

"No heart at all."

The crone was determined to leave.

"Don't get sentimental over a bed."

"I won't," she said as she got out the paper and pen. She could see Michael's face on the percale pillow cover as she wrote.

The crone read aloud over Tecla's shoulder. "Dearest Michael, I shall not be back. Ever. I am taking the lover that you accused me of having so long ago. The one that you insisted was there all during my good looking years. The one you insisted would throw me out if he knew how impossible I was to live with. The one you said must be deaf, dumb, and blind if he thought I was interesting. The one you said would fall over laughing if he saw me in my shriveled up years.

"Michael, the one you threw up in my face everytime I tried to forget him. Let me assure you this last time, my husband, that I never went to him during the hottest nights of my passion, though he was there. I never went to him during the children's fevers, during the children's catastrophes, during the children's celebrations, though he was there. I never went to him because I thought that it mattered if I stayed with you.

"I thought that there was such a thing as fidelity. And, do you know, my husband, there is! I have been faithful, very faithful. For 41 years I have kept this lover wrapped like hope around the barrenness of our marriage. I have not cheated on him once."

Calmly she took the suitcase down from the closet shelf and packed one outfit. Only one. It was the dress that she had bought to be buried in. It will do, she thought. "I want a lover so badly, I can taste him," she said out loud.

But the crone was so excited that for once in her life she was speechless. Her heart was fluttering like a hummingbird at the mouth of the honeysuckle.

Tecla's face, reflected in the dining room table's gleam, was as unwrinkled and as smooth as it had been the day she met Ferdinand. She smiled at her young reporter self and fastened a piece of her hair that had come undone back into the bun on the top of her head.

"41 years," she sighed and moved the fruit bowl into the center of the table.

Abortion Journal

Kate Green

June 4

I keep wondering, is there a baby in my belly? In my dream, I feel it slip out between my legs as I am running, the blood-sac on the dirt. I go back to look at it, the tiny fetus with the large head, insect-eyes that can not close. Realizing it is still alive. I am sullen. It is hot and there is a hole in me that feels good to ache so empty.

June 15

Night. Clouds close in on the city. My little history closes in on me like the heat. Tonight I'm sick, I clock the breathing all the way down to my belly and back. Baby. Knocking in me. Spirit with a hook in this world, caught like a hinge. Oh Blood, answer me clean. I pray for no bodies to ride in through mine. Baby, if you be there, growing your black life in me, how will I ever tell you I shut you off from this world? Trying to grow your body in my blood wheel.

June 16

There is no sky today. The air is thick. All day I wander toward this, the antiseptic hall of women, our backs to the green-tiled walls. We line up the hours alone. I already feel it: finger up my cunt, press and feel from the inside.

Women, American and young—chipped toenail polish, tight jeans, asses with hip-lines of bikini underpants. A Black woman, her hair in fine braids, the only one of us not alone. Her mother sits with her purse in her large lap. Her presence consoles me. Year-old boy plays with a truck making motor noises. I wait. There is no sky. I want to get out of here. I've kept this appointment secret all week. Don't tell Willie, he'll only worry.

A nurse comes in and calls our names: Mary, Katherine, Cora, Anne. We rise obediently and go into separate rooms. I have already pissed in a cup. I have already given my blood to see if I have syphilis or gonorrhea. I take off my jeans and sit on the edge of the examination table. Should have told Willie, should have brought him down here with me. I've overeaten all week and my belly looks fat. It's not that I don't want a baby, just not now. I have fantasies—love and a blue tablecloth, Willie and me in a small apartment over by the lake. But we're not even living together. Don't even know if we want to. Haven't got that far yet. Not ready. Not planning.

I know that, unlike so many, he'd have me keep the baby. "I take care of my own," he said once. "My mother had nine. One more wouldn't make no difference." Come live in my house with Rose and Quinzy. Smell the afternoon smoke of barbeque drift across the summer alley and dance in the evening with nobody home but us. But no, there would be somebody there. Baby, mixed baby, milk chocolate skin, somewhere between your Black and Cherokee daddy, your Welsh and Irish mama.

Monday night I stop at his house. St. Albans like a foreign country, the ghetto, slow St. Paul across the freeway, lilac trees, the ghost of elms now sliced off the earth and the projects like cheap Colorado condominiums. Evening. The hill. We sit in the kitchen. I give him my book, first one off the press this afternoon. His mother, Estalee, says "Now she's big time. Gon' leave you now." *White girl.* "What do these White girls see in you, boy?" Brilliant florescent kitchen, black bare shoulders. Tired eyes.

"How was work?" — "I booked, man." — "You tired?" — "Mmm."

On my way out, I pass the back porch where his cot is stretched out in the dark, where he sleeps during the week when he's not with me but comes home from the factory to eat supper, watch the tube, chat with Rose and the kids, wait for the weekend. Baby, how are things going to change when you have your own place? You could be a father, having already raised two kids, your sister and your nephew.

Voices come back to me. Estalee: "But you ain't going to marry him. He don't make enough money for you." My mother: "What could you possibly have in common?" Jim says blow it all, have the baby, lose your money, wander nameless on the planet. Willie: "Baby, we brand new. We a total mystery."

It makes me sad, how good love is. Clean. Without too many unnecessary murders. Yet we are separate. I'm afraid to come too far into your life, afraid to define, to set up the stage and act out particular lines. It makes me want to move to the mountains, live alone in a cabin, crazy, bolt from the movie of What Does He Do? and How It All Turns Out, to have said, "Yes, I am this life. I have created it." But I crave it, too. Crave it like a name.

This question in my belly makes me burp and feel sick. I lie back on the table, stare up at the nothing white of the ceiling. Feel crying well up deep in my throat and swallow it back down. Why are they taking so goddam long? Just look at the urine. Wave your magic wand. Please God make it No. Maybe I love him. I don't want to think about having an abortion. I don't want to be Wrong. Don't want to have to decide anything, don't want a baby. Don't want to think. Not yet. Please.

Why does everything official happen under florescent lights?

June 17

I pick him up from 3M Friday afternoon in the thunderstorm. I am going to tell him, but it is rush hour and then he goes to sleep. We drive out of the city to my sister's farm, his head against the steamy window, static radio in the gray dusk. By the time he wakes, I've planned it all out in my head, what I will say, how I will word it. He watches me hold back a hot burp, nauseous. "You sick?" — "Not really." — "Morning sickness, huh?" He laughs. — "That's right." — "Girl, I know you lying." — "For real, Willie." —Then: "You're pregnant?"

We ride silent past little farms, green rows of young corn. "What are you going to do?" he says. "What are *we* going to do," I say. All the ride north we talk sad in the car. At first, I pretend I am up in the air. I play at wanting to keep the baby to see what he'll say and simply because it is so real. True fact. And my *body* wants it. We stop at a truck stop for coffee and back in the car, we hold each other. He says, "I don't think it's time. For us. For you. You're young, you got things to do. I can't see you settled down with a kid. I don't know." He looks out the window. Windshield wipers back and forth, back and forth. "If you had it, you'd always hold it against me."

We arrive at the farm after dark, have a cheerful dinner. I don't tell my sister. Hidden secret. Why the shame? Later we walk up the dirt road, sky clearing a space for the moon, wet grass, frogs in the slough. Willie puts his arm around me and we are not alone. He is protective, we play mommy/daddy make-believe. I tell him I've already made the appointment at the clinic. We play at love. Being pregnant makes that clear.

June 19 The Farm

It is afternoon. The flies hum like a pulse through the song of a bird whose insistent tune has wound through me all day. And you, my dark child, who know nothing of earth but my heartbeat and my planetary body, you will never see this late day sun. You will not hear the horse stomp in the pasture or feel the heat on your new face. This sun slants through a stand of trees. Trees do not stop themselves from seeding. Nearby, the bees blend in with the shadows and the dragonflies' papery sound, bees who drive the drones out of the hive in the fall, knowing there is no room for them in winter.

Baby, you have four days to hum in my body before they suck you out of me. I can feel you in me, seven weeks, a fist grabbing me from the inside. Now that you are my body, all my fantasies of you seem shallow and stupid. January, snow baby, dark skin baby. It is so quiet here at the land. The earth is real as a seed. I do not understand my own seeds or living or why I will never hold you outside my belly.

This is as close as you come to earth. Near the door but forever held in me. They say there is something of heaven in that dark curling. To be only in the Mother, only to stay in me, to hear my blood, only to move to my heart. This blue you will never see, your father you will never feel. His hands, his music. He lives well on earth. He would father you, but he knows my movement better than I. He sends you away also and yet I think he doesn't kow how close you are. Single song, hum of fly, afternoon alive, baby in my womb. Life seeks to come through me and I turn away. I am a human animal in shivering space.

June 22

The second day of summer is rainy and hot. We drive down from the four days quiet and green of the farm to the city: neon and thick air, traffic and our separate solitudes. I take a nap, tangle in the damp sheets, dream of blood and water, a bath. I will clean myself, I will bleed. I have never felt so alone. Willie supports the decision but it is finally mine. It is me, my body. Woman body. He does feel the sadness though, and I feel it also—the impossibility of our loving. The love and caring are real; a shared life, a future, a family would be difficult. This baby, this abortion has brought me back from a thousand fantasies of how we could ever come together. I think we both see the huge difference in what we want for our lives.

I keep feeling my life must change because of this. I can't hold it to anything, any of the traditional ties: house, man, baby. Which makes me want to fly out of here, go live in Mexico, South America. Anywhere. Run from myself. I would be back though, seeing my friends and family even more nested, day by day. I am not there yet. No baby, no kitchen, no fifty-years bed. I want to plant something other than a baby. I grew this possibility with my own desires. Can't I plant something else where that desire is a hole in myself?

You see, I can't deny the spirit of this baby, even if it is only eight weeks in my belly. I know it isn't natural to cut it out, to stop the natural growth. Yes it is my choice. Yes I have the right to choose for my body but it will always be my loss. That is all the further I can get with this.

June 23 Abortion Clinic

Bright hot day. Radio on in blue office. Hum of air-conditioner. Willie said he'd come with me today, but I said no, don't bother. One more GYN exam, one more long morning in a waiting room. Now I wish he'd come, wish I could *feel* what I'm feeling. Everything here denies the intensity of having an abortion. Christine, this morning, far away: *don't make such a big deal out of it.* The nurse, taking my blood: *it's not such a melodrama.* Stupid, fucking radio and clinic waiting room filled with magazines with Farrah Fawcett on the cover. In a few hours my body will be mine again. I feel pregnant to the edges of my skin. But now I have begun to shut it down, not to feel pain.

I think of all the times I've sat in a doctor's office, waiting for word about my female body. Years of Planned Parenthood, the pill, IUD insertions, having them pulled out, infections, pap smears, the one that came back *danger*, the biopsies and pathology reports, the cancer operation, how I wept on the white-sheeted table in Boston, wept for Anne's suicide, for lonely sex, for hours in rooms of women and clocks, waiting. That is how I feel today. Another in a series of days that make up my body's history. All the important events of my life focus on my sexuality.

But I can't relate to the "baby" anymore. Is it real? In a couple of hours, they will suck it out of me. I will walk out into the hot day, my body freed from this tie and I can sail out to the west coast and not even touch down. Now I see the heaviness, the weight of this, is not in the pregnancy aborted but in keeping the baby and raising it. The sadness is that it isn't time to have a baby at all, even when my body brims with it.

June 24

Last night I called him. Midnight, he'd just gotten off work. It's over, I told him, crouched naked in the dark. He wouldn't talk so I asked him how he felt. "Lost and angry," he said. "Left out." Kept talking about it being the right choice. *It's ok.*

Me, blank, tired. It happened to someone else. The vacuum machine was chrome and clean, it whirred when it sucked and I couldn't breathe. "There, there," the doctor said. "All done. All over." Recovery room afterward, women in reclining chairs with pink blankets. I pulled my blanket over my head. One woman moaned. They brought us orange juice and cookies. All done. It didn't happen. It never happened. Good as new. Invisible, erased event.

The spirit was not insistent. I sent her back to the other shore. I kept thinking of Bly's seal poem through the painful jolt of my whole skin, as I broke into sweat and breath, riding the fear, " . . . goodbye brother," *goodbye sister*, "die in the sound of waves, forgive us if we have killed you, long live your race, your inner-tube race, so uncomfortable on land, so comfortable in the ocean. Be comfortable in death then, where the sand will be out of your nostrils and you can swim in long loops through the pure death, ducking under as assassinations break above you."

Unnamed spirit, *not, no,* spirit I called in with my fantasies and my longing, you exist now in my huge mother body which monthly sends a white-stone egg down from my natural mind, with the moon, each month, a possible life. You were a little more possible. But in this age, where the choice was given me, I chose no. Today I stand in a new body, not the one I had before the pregnancy or during, but something new. I will always carry the scar of your absence.

Afterwards, I went out into the humid day, stood in line at the dark drugstore on Franklin, waited for the tetracycline, waited for the bus on the corner where the city was happening as usual.

June 25

My body returns to its own concerns. No more tug in my

stomach or air belching out of me all day. No more pressing on my bladder, my breasts grow smaller. They are muscular, soft and of themselves. No more swell and tender when I lie on my side at night, listening to the hum of the air-conditioner from the window next door. In my head rises everything I have ever known about being female, having a body.

Patty: "I went in for the abortion but the baby was too insistent and I had to let him stay."

Candy: "I wanted it. I wanted it. I tried to get pregnant for three years. He wanted me to have an abortion, but I kept my baby. And the father is 'water through my hands, / water on my heart.' "

Meridel: "I wanted a child so I stole the seed of a man and bore a girl-child onto the raging planet. Remember this—there are no more fathers. There are no more fathers."

Adrienne: *"all the fathers are crying: My son is mine!"*

Mother: "Don't ever have an abortion. Your baby would be so wonderful. So many people can't have kids. Someone would love your baby."

Mahri: "Now Tara, I called her in. I called her and she came. I know the night I conceived. I remember Joe saying I was never so open as that night. He won't even come to look at her now. And when Jessie was born and his head was crowning, I shouted, 'His hair! His hair!' and I felt it with my hands. 'What color is it?' And when he came out with his straight black hair and it was obvious that his father wasn't Black, Joe said, 'You mean to tell me you didn't even know who the father of the baby was? You disgust me.' "

Carla: "So I flew to New York and was home that night. Don't ever, ever tell anyone. I wouldn't want him to know." And two years later, after having a child, her second child stillborn, she wrote to me: "My baby died in me. I felt my own breath stop, my blood go stale, my body so deaf to his death in me, I couldn't cough him out for two days. Noon of the third day, I cried my son out and laid him in the quiet desert. Now I sing to my husband's skin. We talk of planting."

Pat: "Snake man, doctorman come to scoop you out with his knives and 'Death is never a woman.' "

Anne: "Or say what you meant, / you coward ... this baby that I bleed."

Hysterectomies: Evie, Jane. Masectomies: JoAnn, cysts and lumps, Kathy, Irene, my mother, cones, me, culposcopies, abortions, Pat, Carol (three), Susan, Holly, Marcia, Jenné , Carla—

Me: "I don't think I could ever have an abortion."

Mary: "To me it was just like having a tooth pulled. Nothing more. A medical procedure. I felt no emotion."

Asha: "A year after my abortion, one night I was violently sick and I shook and sweated and threw up. Later, my husband said to me, 'Now you've finally finished your abortion.' "

Etheridge: "I guess my come is dead. All those years of drugs and shit and booze."

Adoptions: Judy, Marilyn, Nancy, McAnally.

Etheridge: "Here's my advice to you. Don't be afraid to have a family."

The doctor, just before my abortion, as I lay in the stirrups under the florescent lights, "I see you've had a cone biopsy. You know that isn't far away from cancer. Well, what *are* your plans for having a family? *Don't defer forever.*" And the assistants holding tubes and my hands, talking about nursing their children, "I had to get up every two hours with Sarah," and me wanting to scream Shut up! Shut Up! Can't you understand I am here, this is real, I am dying?

First Period / contraceptives / impotence in men / casual sex with strangers / empty sex / cold sex / celibacy and masturbation / getting it down with my hands / my lesbian sisters / my infatuation with other women / rape / forced sex / unhappy sex / lovely amazing celestial love-making sex / missed periods / waiting / stirrups and speculums / waiting / rubber fingers / biopsies and cauterizations / yeast infections / IUD infections / syphilis and gonorrhea / warts / pimples / sore dry cunt from fucking too long / becoming aware of ovulation / cramps / cleansing / celebration of the moon / synchronization of periods with women friends / abortion / stillborn / miscarriage / nursing / mama / mama / delivery / fetus / let the miracle happen / you have the right to choose for your own body / and thousands of years of law, by family, by church, by state and king and all of them men, crying *"My son is mine!"*

June 26

Again it is sunny. It isn't right to feel good and happy. I want to cry. It has come into my throat a few times but I have not cried. Sad how it all evades me. No ceremony, no rite of passage for an abortion.

Yesterday, Willie came over with the money for the abortion. "His half." He walked in, pulled out his wallet, threw the bills down on the table. A hundred bucks. I felt cheap: womb, crime, woman unclean. "Baby, don't treat me like that," I said. Then he yelled, "Well, what did any of it have to do with me. You didn't even want me to come. Here's your fucking money." Realizing later I had the act of the abortion itself to focus my feelings on while he's had nothing at all. It was his child, too. I tried to comfort him, but he pulled back and sat on the front steps all morning staring at the street.

Last night in the evening heat and stillness, Christine and I drove by the Lake Harriet bandstand where a swing band in red sportcoats played old dance music that swelled out over the water. The sky grew pink, then dark, and the city lights came on. I felt then that I was very far away from the city, that it didn't exist as a place to have a life in. It was only a spot on the planet and I rose higher and higher, away from all that is human and ongoing and hovered like a darkness over my earthly life.

******

Tonight, Carla calls from Santa Fe to say she gave birth to a nine pound boy. The birth happened about two hours after my abortion.

June 30

Sorrow leaves my body. Now all that remains is a hole and the curious attitude of continuance, a flatness where the daily business of breath and survival, of daylight and dinner, of freeway and skin, the business of Being fills me in. I talked to Mom and Dad on the phone, mentioning nothing of this. Afterwards, I felt such anger, I couldn't place it, outside me or inside. I tore at space, tried to rip the air with slammed doors, scratching arm movements, to tear or grip something in the emptiness. I fell into myself, crazy, crying and sweeping, crying and tearing up papers and newspapers, gasping and breathing hard. Cleaning the house, sobbing, scrubbing the dishes, my hair wet and thick in my face, my throat filled with air, choking me. Something in my gut tearing out of me and I had no way to call it by name —death or loss, love or memory, nothing— only the welling up, a wave of myself spilling out of control. *Help me. Help.* Watch me scream this quiet Sunday into how I hurt like a cut in my breath, this green morning. I am broken, mama. I am broken and healing. I am my own mother now that all my mother-energy bleeds out of my body, my woman-river of hormones turning back like a tide pulled out to sea. Mother, I break and heal. I hurt to say, "I make my life." No one can hold me now.

Later Willie and I walk in the park. I let him into me in a new way. "Now that our love has made a baby," he says. "I like to walk next to you and feel your breasts rubbing against my arm." We are closer now. Almost like brother and sister, but sexual. The fetus is gone, but there is a bond of our bodies that remains.

Down by the lake, Sunday afternoon. A city afternoon. Families, Black and White and Chicano, splashing and yelling in the water-light. I regard the babies, especially the Black and mixed babies. Willie says, "We're all mulatto." I watch them but I am past the want I used to have, that longing for what seemed impossible. I hold his hand. We stand in the brown water, squint into the sun.

The day dissolves. Later with the rain spinning torrents at the screens, I rock and moan for him to come into me. His fingers slide between my legs, a deep and hurting desire. We can't make love. The doctor said no relations for ten days. We hold each other, stroke our genitals and sweat in the night of rain.

(June 1977—October, 1979)

A War Dream

Warren Schmidt

I WAS ON THE White House lawn, in the back yard, and I was looking at the surrounding countryside. There were no buildings or streets. Beyond the lawn was tall grass and brush and in the distance the forest, misty in the twilight, a faint rust color above the trees from the setting sun. A glowing white horse galloped into the trees. The land looked like what I had seen between Quang Tri and Hue, the way it looks a few miles in from the coast before the hills begin. I could hear sniper fire from the forest; the usual intermittent kind, one or two shots an hour from ancient French rifles which never hit anyone—background music, the barking of dogs as you come into a strange neighborhood. John Kennedy was across the lawn. He was dressed like a farmer and he was square dancing by himself.

On the lawn were rows of long buffet tables covered by white table cloths with plates of chicken legs and bowls of wild rice on them. Other soldiers and I stood or walked amid the tables as we talked and ate. Some of us were dressed in army uniforms cut like tuxedos and others in high school band uniforms.

Lady Bird Johnson was across the table from me. When she talked sparks came from her mouth, benign toy Tommy gun sparks. She had garden tools for hands.

My first sergeant edged up to me. He was a bowlegged little man with a shriveled alcoholic face and a crew cut. He had an olive drab frisbee for a plate.

"Hi sarg."

"Hi. I'm dead."

"I know."

"Boy, you sure look natural," someone near us said and someone else laughed.

"Hurt ya much?" I asked.

"Didn't feel like I thought it would," the sergeant said, as we started to stroll alongside the table. "Fuckin' mortars. I could feel those pellets spinning inside me. But it didn't hurt. Smelled the blood in my nose but it didn't hurt. It was like you were in—it was in slow motion. Everything was in slow motion and you had that funny feeling—ya know, those elevator feelings in your stomach. Like you were fallin' back but you'd never hit. It was a nice feeling. Once you got used to it. It's nice. You're not scared. . . . And I kept fallin' and I kept thinkin' 'What the hell's the use.' Ya know what I mean? I mean, who cares. . . . Ya know what I mean? . . . Ya know what I mean?"

"Well, yeah, sort of."

We were nearing a zinc coffin at the end of the table. A soldier wearing a high school band uniform—my first sergeant and I were wearing the army uniforms cut like tuxedos—walked along with us. He ate a drumstick from the sergeant's frisbee, bone and all.

"It was nice," the sergeant said. "Not bad, not scary. It—it was nice. It was nice. It really was." The inside of the coffin was upholstered in blue satin. He got into the coffin and sat up in it. "Ya don't have to bust your ass anymore. Worry about things." Then he said, vehemently, as if he were addressing himself, "Hey, how come you're not a success? How come you're a flunky sergeant in the army? How come you look like nothin'? What's Kant's *dick* and *sik* about anyway?"

"*Ding an sich*," I corrected.

"Well, who cares! What does it matter? I don't have to do that stuff. I'm dead. The pressure's off. I'm fuckin' dead, dickhead! Wake the fuck up! Right and wrong. Who cares. . . . It's nice. Not scary."

He reached down to the lever sticking out of the satin upholstery and threw the coffin into gear and drove off across the lawn and into the tall grass, parting the grass as if it was hair, then gained speed and plowed through it like a motor boat.

The soldier wearing the band uniform began speaking to me. His voice was the sound of a pinball machine with a border state accent—Tennessee, I think. We talked about being home and I could see the sergeant's coffin fishtailing near the forest. The sound of the sniper shots clustered around him. The soldier's voice changed from the pinball machine noises to a human voice.

"I'm so tired all the time," he said.

"Me too," I said.

"Sleep half the day. Fell alseep at my girl's last night watching tv. Never did that before."

"I think it's the change in climate. It'll go away. I hope."

"It better."

"I take a lot'a naps. Doesn't seem to help much, though."

A voice came from behind and above me, a commanding voice, "YOU KNOW HOW TO TAKE A NAP, SON?"

I turned and looked up into the face of President Lyndon Johnson. He was hunched over me like a giant crow. He waited for an answer, breathing heavily through his nose, the air whistling through the hair in his nostrils.

"Yea—Yes, Mister President."

"HOW DO YOU TAKE A NAP?"

"Well . . . lay down. Take my shoes off first. And lay down. On my bed."

"THAT'S NOT THE WAY. YOU GET ON YOUR JAMMIES. AND COVER UP. PULL 'EM WAY UP THERE. YOU GOT'TA LET THE SLEEP SNEAK UP ON YA. UNDERSTAND?"

"Yes, Mister President."

"Yes, Mister President," said the soldier I had been talking to.

An aide ran up to the president and showed him two large raw onions.

"How 'bout these babies!" the aide said.

The President turned to me and put his hand on my shoulder, "PROUD OF YOU SON."

And he hurried away with the aide. Soldiers had crowded around the hear the conversation. They looked at me.

"Bug out!" someone yelled from far away. And we turned to his voice and saw him in fatigues running toward us through the grass.

"Bug out! Bug out! Bug the fuck out!"

We stood there watching the yelling soldier running toward us. Then something terrible and shrieking was coming down from the sky and we looked up and were afraid. I felt a sudden rush of heat against me and the ground did a slow twitch like it was made of rubber and the White House wobbled and the lawn bulged up forming a little hill and tables and soldiers slid off the hill and the hill grew and exploded into a swirling of dirt and tables and screaming young men. I could see revolving in the swirl the dismembered arms and legs of giant dolls, clean and whole and then a human leg was thrown out of the swirl in my direction and sailed slowly, sedately by me, bloody and oozy at the thigh and charred crisp at the foot, the boot aflame, like a wounded ship.

And the swirling fell to the ground and the ground was black and smoldering and humped with debris. The smell of sulfur hung in the air. The trees in the yard were leafless. The back of the White House was scorched. Wounded men and broken dolls whimpered on the ground. A hideous thing with wings, part pheasant and part old woman fluttered and flopped among them, looking for her young. And I stood there untouched and Lyndon Johnson was looking down from his window and crying.

Snow

Mary Logue

A beautiful snow falls on a bed,
Amazing the man and woman there.
It falls between them and over them where
Just before they lay close and naked.
 Philip Dacey

S NOW SWARMED through the air and over the free-way. The tires
made no sound as they moved over the road and in the car, Anne
and Nathan were silent. Anne stared out the window and thought of
a dust storm in the desert, though snow, being lighter than sand, flew
up higher, billowed up over the cars. The snow, as it drifted into piles
on the sides of the road, was so clean, rows of muslin sheets layed out
to dry. Soon women, round and ruddy, with scarves tied over their
hair, would come and fold them all up.

"Is the driving all right?" she asked Nathan, realizing she could
barely make out the cars in front of them.

"It's a bit slippery, but we're almost there. It's this exit, isn't it?"

When they pulled up in front of Anne's house, the silence held
until she couldn't stand it anymore and said, "Well, what would you
like to do?"

"I'd like to come in and see your place." He turned off the car.

"Oh, Nathan, it's late. Why don't you come over to see it another
day?"

"Because I don't feel like leaving. We haven't even talked, just
seen a movie and had a drink. I really need to talk to you. You're the
only one who can understand."

"You won't give anyone else a chance."

"Let me come up for a while, maybe the snow will let up."

"OK, but just for a while." Pushing open the car door, she saw
the snow had drifted over the sidewalk until it was impossible to find
it. She pulled her hood up and ran to the door.

Once in her apartment she tried to relax with Nathan, throwing
pillows on the floor for them to lean on. Maybe there were things
they should talk out; she hadn't seen him for close to two weeks.

"How are your folks?" she asked, sitting on the floor, her back
against the bed.

"Oh, pretty good. I think they feel bad about us."

"Yeah, I've thought of that. It always mattered to me what they

71

thought of me. I guess I was surprised when I realized they liked me."

"I've been spending a lot of time out there. They haven't said anything but I know they must be thinking—the only time we see him is when things go wrong." He stretched out on the floor, folding his arms behind his head, "My mom and I were washing the dishes together the other night and we started talking over everything. My dad just ignores it, at least my mom will talk about it with me. She turned to me and said, 'I'd like to say that Anne wasn't good enough for you . . .' I started to protest when she added 'but it wouldn't be true."

Anne looked down and started unlacing her boots, "I don't know if that makes me feel good or bad."

He moved over and sat next to her, stroking her heavy brown hair with his hand, playing with it. It had always fascinated him, straight and long. He would pull it back out of her face, after they made love, and braid it, sometimes little braids all over her head or more simply one fat one down her back. It used to soothe her, but now she disliked him touching it.

"I've been thinking of getting it cut, real short and maybe henna it."

"Why?"

"For a change. I'm tired of it."

As if to protect it, he grabbed her hair at the back of her neck, "If you do that, why don't you give me the hair.

She laughed, "Oh, come on. That's a little too sentimental for you."

"No, you'd be surprised how sentimental I've become. The house is haunting me, everything is you. I can remember buying it with you. You should still be there. Sometimes at night I think you are, I hear you down in the kitchen and I think all I have to do is wait. She's probably getting something to eat and she'll be up in a few minutes. It's a nice thought."

"I think it'd be good for you to sell the house or at least rent it out to someone else. Maybe even share it — get a room-mate."

"I've been thinking about it but . . . it seems so final. I guess I keep hoping."

Anne wound her hair around her hand, forming a bun at the nape of her neck, "Hope is fatal, you know."

"Well, then, I hope I die from it." He turned away.

"Hey. I was kidding. Come on, didn't we agree that when we were together we would try to be happy." She let her hair fall down her back when she reached out to him.

"Right. Happy. Snap out of what I'm feeling, what I've been feeling for weeks and be happy for your sake. God, Anne, what do you think I am?"

"Nothing more than you." She stared at him.

"Sometimes I want you so bad, I feel it here," he grabbed his crotch, "here," his chest, "and even in my hands, an ache for you." He took her by the arms, pulled her close and kissed her. Near him his smell hit her, only he smelled like that; blindfolded, confronted with hundreds of men, she would recognize him. An earth smell, not flowery, more like leaves that have spent a winter under snow and are ready for spring, a growing smell.

"Nathan, I don't want this."

"Well, I do. When do I get what I want? Why do you dictate everything?"

She kicked out her legs and spread them apart on the rug, "OK, go ahead. Just do it." Leaning back on the bed, she closed her eyes. Silence, then she felt him unbuttoning her shirt. "No, no need for that. Make it what you're talking about." She unbuckled her pants.

Nathan continued unbuttoning her shirt and reached in for a breast. Gently, like he was touching a seedling, he nudged it back and forth. Kissing her neck, he whispered, "We could make it so good."

Anne lifted his chin, forcing him to look at her, "This is crazy."

"Just let go. Let go of what you think should happen." He finished unbuttoning her shirt and took it off. She looked down at her two nipples; they looked happy to see Nathan, standing at attention, no disguising that. He took them in his hands and held them like they were cupped water, then bent down and kissed them. "I'm going to turn out the light."

She moved up on to the bed. Laying back, she decided she wouldn't do much, but let it happen to her, as there seemed no way out of it. Nathan, standing at the foot of the bed, took his shirt off. With his upper torso bare and his pants hanging around his hips, he looked like a peasant. She had always wondered if he had some gypsy blood in him, he was so dark and hairy.

"Lift your feet up." He grabbed the bottom of her pants and pulled them off. She was naked but she didn't feel vulnerable. They had spent more time together naked, than clothed. "Now spread your legs apart."

He fell on her and as their skins touched, moving against each other, she realized she hadn't felt her own body for a long time. In isolation, it left its imprint on nothing; only against another warmth could she make out its outline.

More than excited she felt accepting; making love with Nathan was like falling back into the steps of a familiar dance. They moved well together, exchanging the lead occassionally and falling back on the bed when the music was over. Opening her eyes, she cautiously glanced at him. An arm lay across his chest, the fingers slightly curled, he was close to sleep.

She hoped that he would sleep. The silence was a comfort. No more arguing or explanations that piled up like snow on top of all their actions.

But watching him closely, his fist clenched and he lifted it to his face, rubbing his eyes. Quickly, Anne closed her eyes and regulated her breath, faking sleep.

"Do you want me to go? I'll go if you do." He was up on an elbow, looking down at her.

"Do you mean it? Don't say it if you don't mean it. — I want you to go."

"Why?"

"I want to be alone." Anne said it into her pillow.

"You're alone all the time."

"I know and I like it. I'm used to it."

"Well, I don't want to be alone, so I'm staying."

"You're a liar." She sat up.

"It wasn't a lie. I just didn't think you would ask me to go and I wanted to hear you asking me to stay. Maybe I would have left then."

"Small chance," she stretched out facing the wall.

The bed rose as he stood up. Listening intently, she could barely hear him walk across the floor.

"This snow just won't quit. I can't go home when it's coming down like this."

"You don't need any excuses, Nathan."

"Well, what do I need?" he strode across the room and pulled her up. "What do I need to get through to you?"

She cringed, gasping at the suddenness of his action, "Don't."

"I wasn't going to hurt you, Anne. I couldn't hurt you. I love you."

"You say that so defensively. Do you think it will change anything?"

"I would never be fool enough to think that," he let go of her. "I guess I think you'll hear me someday."

"Do I seem so far away?"

"Further than you can imagine," he sat down next to her. "Let me stay with you, maybe just sleeping in the same bed will form some connection between us."

She stood up and went into the bathroom to wash. Her red silk robe was hanging above the tub and she put it on. "OK, you can stay. But please, let's go to sleep. I have to get up tomorrow, even though it's Saturday."

When she came back into the room he was already in bed, the sheet pulled up to his chin. She climbed over him. They arranged themselves the way they always slept together, she on the inside, he on the outside. Leaning over to kiss him, she whispered, "Good night."

"Good night."

They lay quiet. Her bed was too small for two people. Anne squeezed up next to the wall, giving Nathan more of the bed, though he, too, was close to the edge. She willed herself to go to sleep, but was conscious of the faint breathing and slight stirs he was making.

"You should have left me sooner." It was said quietly, but with an intenseness behind it like a threat.

She sighed, "You're probably right. I will take the blame for that."

"No blame intended. It would have made it easier."

"For you, but I left you when I could. I couldn't have left you before that."

"Yeah." With this word, he relaxed, moving a little closer to her.

Thinking back on the many times she had tried to leave him, she remembered the tears. They would talk about living apart, becoming friends and she would cry, harsh sobs of fear at being alone. But slowly she pulled him out of her life. On the day she finally left him she didn't cry. Alone in the car she hadn't known where to go. Wanting a totally impersonal place, she ended up at the Shopper's City on 15th Avenue. She looked at tennis shoes, hair clips, gardening tools and cookware for an hour, then left absolved of something.

Out the window she could see the snow was still coming down. In the Bible, they said people would become as pure as the driven snow. She wondered what driven snow was. Maybe to come clean you had to stand in a snow storm and have the snow driven into your body and soul.

Waking early in the morning she stared at Nathan's back, smooth and white, his head tucked down under his shoulder. His black hair was growing long, the curls becoming ringlets that hung down below his shoulders. Before she had always kept it short, making sure it was dripping wet so she could straighten it and cut it evenly.

How long would he sleep? The alarm clock that she set on the floor near the bed read 9:30. They had gone to bed at 3:30. She wanted to lay down again but knew she couldn't drop back to sleep. Sitting on the edge of the bed, she kneaded her muscles. Whenever she had a bad night, because of dreams or drinking, her leg muscles would ache in the morning like growing pains.

Nathan stirred in the bed. She wanted him up and out, "You ready for some breakfast?"

"What time is it?"

"Time to get up." She walked into the kitchen. "I'm going to make pancakes."

"Gee, I'd like to sleep a little longer." He pulled the covers up around his head.

"Nathan, I have things to do. If you want to get up and have breakfast with me, you'll have to do it now, because I'm leaving soon."

"All right."

She had never lived by herself before and her kitchen was a joy to her. Everything was where it should be, the pots and pans hung above the stove. If there were dishes in the sink she was at fault, but she knew they would be done. In a long ashbox near the window the herbs she had planted when she moved in were getting large enough to pick. Heather plants hung in rows down the window, casting a green light into the kitchen.

A kitchen always seemed like the center of a house to her. Even though she had a work table in the bedroom, she often sketched at the kitchen counter. Ideas would come to her as she ate and she learned to have a pad available.

She put a pan of water on for tea —no coffee today, it would only aggravate her lack of sleep— and mixed up the pancake batter.

"I like this place. You've got it fixed up real nice. It's changed so much since you first moved in." Nathan leaned in the doorway, watching her.

"Yeah, it's beginning to feel like it is my place. I like all the windows. Sun all day long."

"Do you need anything? I've still got most of the furniture."

"Well, I don't know. What are your plans? Are you going to stay at the house for awhile?"

"Yeah, it's a bit expensive just for me but I haven't had the energy to look for another place." He walked over and put his arms around her waist, his chin resting on her shoulder.

"Why don't you set the table? The dishes are up in that cupboard." She poured in the first pancake, watching the edges rise up and bubble. "Oh, one thing I want, I forgot my old blue teapot. It's up in the buffet in the living room. I've been having to make tea in a pan, which takes away from the ritual."

Looking out the window, Nathan said, "I'd say we got seven inches last night."

"Are you going to have any trouble getting your car out?"

"No, I have sand and a shovel in the trunk."

After they had eaten, Nathan cleared the dishes away and got ready to go, while she sat drinking her tea and doodling.

"You know my show is coming up," she said.

"Right, it's next Thursday, isn't it?"

"Yeah."

"Do you have everything ready?"

"No. I've got a hat and a blouse to finish. Do you want to see the wall-hanging I've done?" She led him into the small nook off the bedroom that she used as her work room. Shelves went from floor to ceiling on two of the walls and hanging next to the window was her latest work, done all in old and new satin. She had gone to the Goodwill and found three old satin dresses; the rich, faded fabric formed the backdrop of the piece with some new satin added over it for accent.

Nathan didn't say anything at first, just stood, weight on his left leg, arms folded over his chest and stared.

"I really like it. It's good." He walked up closer to it, running his fingers over the fabric, "It reminds me of that shirt you made me. You used some of the same colors."

"That shirt wasn't satin, though, it was just cotton."

"Yeah, but the colors were the same, blue and green with a touch of red." She had given him the shirt for his birthday two years before. It was the first piece she had totally designed herself.

As she walked him to the door, he said, "Maybe I should stay and see that you get out all right."

"No, I've got a few things I should finish up here before I go."

"Thanks for breakfast."

"Thanks for the movie last night."

"Anne," he stopped at the door.

"Look it, I'll talk to you in awhile. Let me call you this time, OK?"

"I try to wait, but it's so hard."

She put her hands on his shoulders, "It'll be all right. It will get easier. It has to."

Standing on tiptoe she kissed him gently on the mouth, a kiss he ignored as he said, "I'm not getting used to it."

"Nathan, don't start that again. Please. Kiss me and leave."

"There's nothing I can do?"

"Not right now."

He kissed her, a hungry kiss which she pulled out of, "Good-by."

"Good-by."

She stripped the sheets off the bed, leaving them piled up in the middle of the floor and went into the kitchen to have another cup of tea. Tired, she stared at the snow. If she blanked her mind of everything, didn't let Nathan or work in, maybe the snow would seep in through her eyes and her brain would be a snow storm. She would be found with acute frost-bite of the inner sanctum. But Nathan would not stay out. Even with her mind filled with snow, he came tracking up, persistent as ever.

She remembered waking to the sound of Nathan gritting his teeth in the night. She reached over and cupped his chin in her hand and massaged it, trying to loosen it up. He never woke up when she tried to unclench his jaws; so absorbed in his sleep that he didn't feel it. Trying to get away from her hand, he turned his head. He was perspiring lightly and she wiped his forehead, pushing the curls off his face. At night, he reminded her of a child, he must have been beautiful when he was young. No wonder his mother was sad they had broken up, no one to take care of her boy anymore. There did well up in her an urge to make everything better, to wake him up and tell him she would move back but it didn't last long. Even though she loved him, or maybe because she loved him, it was too late to go back.

Pulling herself away from the night she returned again to the snow. White, a deep white, drifts full of it. Maybe she would try designing something all in white, a long robe, a flowing dress; at first glance, it would appear to be one piece but a closer examination would disclose it was white on white, overlappings, tucks and hidden pockets. She could hear her mother saying that white was impractical, impossible to keep clean, but her mother, raised in a motherless family during the depression, always saw objects as equal to the work they demanded and the wear they gave. Her mother, like her lovers, was a small voice she carried around inside her head, referring to her at moments of stress.

"Mother, what should I do about Nathan?"

"Well, you can either be firm about not seeing him or you can resort to meanness," a pause as if there were a question of which it would be. "It's up to you."

"But what makes it hard is the growing realization that I still love him, that I care about him and hate to see him so miserable. I don't understand why it has changed."

Sometimes she tried to pinpoint the exact moment when their relationship had changed. She saw her life with Nathan as a long walk up a mountain. For so many years she had been pulling him up one side of the slope, wanting their love to work more than he did. Then at some moment it turned: perhaps she was standing in front of the mirror, pinning her hair up, and she felt his eyes on her, found them in the mirror and saw that they were staring at nothing. She began to wonder why she had cared so much and relaxed her hold on him. Without her persistence, they had tumbled down the other side of the mountain, years faster than it had taken to go up.

The phone rang in the other room, surprising her as it broke the silence. She walked to the phone, waiting until it rang a second time before lifting it up, a superstition of hers never to appear anxious. She sat down on the end of the bed, "Hello."

"Hi." His voice jarred her.

"Oh, it's you. What do you want?"

"I just called to see if you had made plans for before the opening. I thought we might have dinner."

"Before the opening? I'm sorry but Jenny and I made plans. We're going to dress each other up and have dinner together."

"Yeah, well I thought maybe . . ." His voice grew faint as if he were backing away from the receiver.

"Well, it was a nice idea."

"Anne, would you have gone out to dinner with me, if you hadn't been doing something with Jenny?"

He always pushed everything to the limit, wanted to know all. "How do you expect me to know?" she snapped, then smoothing out the back of her hand and taking a deep breath, she said, "Hey, I'm sorry I've been so short with you. I guess I'm still a little upset about last night. Nathan, it's really hard for me to know. You're beginning to 'if', too."

"If?"

"You know, like kids, if you had a million dollars what would you do with it? I might not have gone out with you. I guess, I don't trust you."

"So now you don't trust me. We barely begin to get closer together and you don't trust me. Why?"

"Because you lied to me last night. You've never lied to me before."

"Listen, I might have lied to you out right, but you lied, too. You lied with your body. You held back, when you wanted more. You lied to yourself."

"Why do you call me to ask me out to dinner when you feel that way about me?"

"Because I still love you." He hung up.

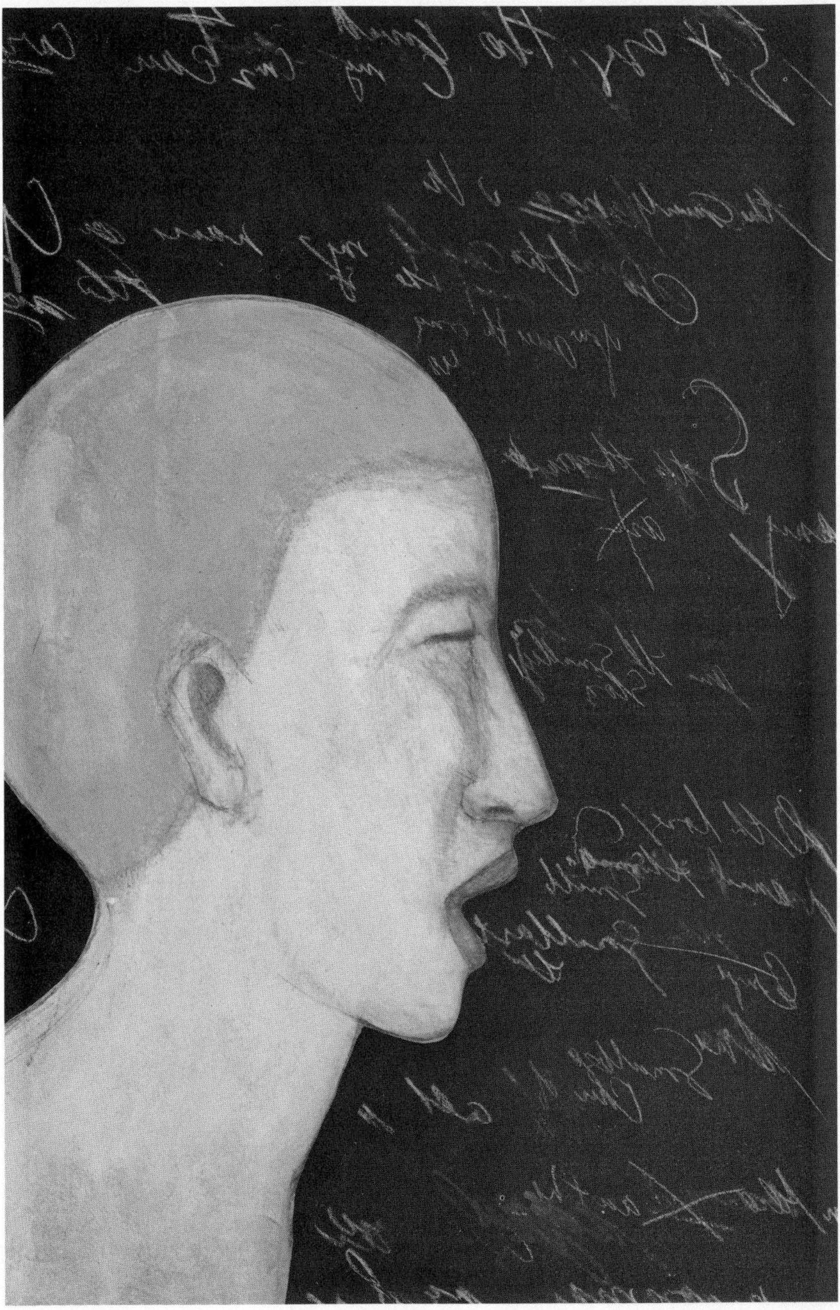

Microwaves Passing Through
An Aside At The Premier
Performance Of
Having Good Fun
At A Tibetan Funeral

R Bartkowech

D URING THE early passages of the first act, I could not help but notice that up on the balcony, in the dim glow of the emergency exit lights, the fuzzy-wuzzies atop Madame Buchard's elegant headdress were standing straight up, their little limbs stretched out taut, electrified by some invisible force. A few minutes into the third scene, the madame leaps to her feet and begins applauding, the slapping of her sweaty hands echoing round and round the opera house, stopping the actors dead in their tracks. Now, with her arms flung open as if ready to catch a baby thrown from a burning building, she is lit up in the spotlight.

"Would that I were young again, or the sands remained unmoving in my lover's unimpassioned eyes ! Then the clear spring pools calling down the nightingale to fill its thirst, and the willow-beast bouncing bumba-bumba across the moonlit hills... But why feed these mangled roots? And why this clumsy promenade through the stench of borrowed time?"

Madame Buchard has a dizzy spell and has to sit down. The spotlight swings back to stage center. Standing behind a rectangular wooden box, an actor wearing a black tuxedo and white gloves is applauding and screaming, "Bravo! Bravo!" Another actor in similar attire is sitting up in the casket, his opera glasses still trained on the balcony. There's a regular hub-bub going on up there. A body is being carried out through the balcony's private curtain.

The man in the casket passes his opera glasses to the attendant and then turns to the audience.

"Soon, everyone will be celebrating. The elevator is working perfectly. Given the amount of property I have left behind, this should turn into a veritable fat Tuesday. What a soufflé must have fluffed up in my ex-wife's petite frontal lobes when she found out that only days after she had quit me I had quit myself. Perhaps she'll sneak in anyway. We are all scavengers. It's so comfortable to be huddled together where the action is. A Yugoslavian prince will arrive shortly with his most beautiful harem. Everyone will be fricassied in minutes."

An usher with a tiny flashlight steps up out of the orchestra pit. He walks down the aisle and stops at row thirty-five. The bulb flashes on and off, lighting up his white glove. He's signalling for me. I excuse myself and make my way slowly toward the aisle. Twelve people have to move their knees and pull their feet under their seats. They are very annoyed. I smile politely.

As the usher leads me toward the lobby, the audience begins laughing hysterically. I stop and turn around. The actor is trying to control himself in the casket, his hands clutching the golden handles on the sides of the box. His head's shaking, and his eyes and tongue are popping out. He looks like a salamander who's just been castrated and dunked in a vat of bubbling fondue. Now his hair stands up on end, and he falls backward, crashing down into his final position.

I follow my escort through the lobby, down a spiral staircase, and along a dark corridor which seems to be heading back in the direction of the stage. He motions with his white glove.

"Hurry!" he says. "Soon, everyone will be celebrating!"

An out of order sign is hanging across the bottom of the escalator. I have to jump over the chain and run up the grated, metal steps. At the top, the usher is waiting, bent slightly forward at the waist, his right arm extended, his hand indicating the proper door.

"This way, sir!"

In the dressing room, the tails are draped over the back of the chair. My gloves are on the dresser. I put on a starchy, white shirt and fasten it at the neck. He helps me with the jacket.

Backstage I can see the elaborate structural supports for the lighting and the sets, the wooden struts crossing each other in endlessly repeating patterns. One of the actors has just gotten into the coffin and closed the lid on himself. The tails from his tuxedo are caught and hang down the side of the box. An attendant goes over, lifts the lid, tucks the tails in and slams the coffin shut. People are bursting their sides.

A third actor enters from stage right, lights several candles around the Tibetan catafalque and steps to the footlights right above the orchestra pit. He is about to begin his soliloquy, but something is wrong. He's trembling. There's a strange twitch in the back of his neck. An alert stage-hand closes the curtain as if this were the end of the scene.

No sooner is the curtain drawn than the actor spins around and falls flat on his face, his arms stretched out like a traffic cop signalling with the palms of his white gloves for everyone to stop. The crew pulls him off and I'm shoved out to his position. I'm almost an exact double. The audience will have no idea of what's going on.

Now the curtain slowly rises, the footlights glistening, reflecting off my shoes, off the knife-edge pleats in my trousers, off the silver dust which has been sprayed into my hair, off my white gloves which I raise in the air for silence.

Madame Buchard must have had to leave early. Her balcony has already been filled by others. It's a packed house. People are standing in the aisles and all along the back of the theatre. There can't be a soul left in the city.

"How can we help but be drawn to this place? Our little daddy's wallet intermezzo, cleaved like a tit from its anything but scanty flight — surely there might be something left for *us*! Ah hah! Listen now as our recently departed turns over in his casket!" (Dead silence.) "Well, perhaps my prompter can explain. An understudy has such little time to prepare for stardom."

The prompter enters stage left, holding open a scroll of the script.

"Pssst! No! No! It's, 'Well, perchance thy chomper plans in vain. A misunderstanding has left such little to dine on. Fanfare of boredom! Chompers held open in a cage bereft of squid or escargot!'"

"Oh yes. I stand corrected. Yet such contingency does not forestall our joy. We are trembling. We are drooling."

"Pssst! Pssst! You stand corrected. Yet such ... such ... "

The prompter begins trembling and drooling, then he collapses in a pile of twitching flesh and is carried off. After everyone quiets down, I continue.

"We cannot be protected. 'Tis true. Even now the ushers are stepping from the blackness of the orchestra pit with their teensy-weensy flashlights. They stop at the end of your row and they signal for you. You excuse yourself and smile. People get annoyed. There you go, one by one, off to the lobby, down the spiral staircase, and through the long, unlit corridors. You push the button for the elevator, but it's not working. You stand on the grated, metal steps of the mechanical stairway; by the hundreds you are drawn slowly, smoothly up to your rooms where you dress for la grande bouffe. The audience is thinning out like crazy. The wings are packed. People are laughing and whooping it up in anticipation. Everyone's coming out from stage right and left.

We are dancing and hugging, singing and swaying. The sets are pushed off the edge of the stage and crash down into the darkness. Around the periphery of the crowd, the Yugoslavian prince's harem is fast put to pleasure, the floor of the stage bouncing bumba-bumba and the curtain swaying with the sighs of swollen lovers. Mrs. Tebnahsech opens the glass door of the box atop the casket. She puts a chicken in and sets the dial for thirteen seconds. A buzzer goes off the door pops open and it's roast chicken time for everybody! Sloppy good! Now baked potatoes in four seconds! Spirits are going up, up! Port Salut fondue in *two seconds*! Wine, women, and song! Hurrah! Braised lobster in thirty-seven hundreths of a second! Voila! People are doing the lip-smacking crustacean wobble! An entire seventy-five pound pig no fuss no bother one thousandth of a second! The hambone shake! We're having a *really* good time! We're drooling food!

Suddenly we hear a strange clatter, something out of place. Everyone lifts their opera glasses and stares out into the shadows of the empty theatre. Someone, somewhere is applauding. But it's a muted sort of clapping, echoing round and round off the walls and the high domed ceiling. Then one by one we notice, up on the highest center balcony, a pair of white gloves slapping into one another, palm to palm, very proper. An alert stage-hand spins one of the spotlights up there. Two white gloves swing alone through the air, little wings without a body, clapping, clapping.

The woman to my right starts trembling and falls to the floor. People all around me are having spasms and collapsing. And we'll keep dropping — till we'll all be singing and swaying and carrying on till we'll all be having such good fun and we won't even notice the play is over."

Cold Birth

Patricia Weaver Francisco

"Cold Birth" is an exerpt from a novel-in-progress concerning a man's attempts to integrate himself with the world. The novel opens in Michigan and follows Yoder, the main character, as he travels across the country, bouncing between friends, family and lovers. His first stop is Maine, where he renews ties with Josh, an old friend from college. Upon arriving, he finds Josh living with Ruthie, a woman he immediately resents and distrusts.

H E HAD BEEN in Maine nearly three weeks before he saw a birth. Josh and Ruth were up most of the night with the pregnant cow. Drunk on wine, he had remained inside, picking out tunes on his guitar late into the night. Josh woke him at five o'clock, shouting up the stairs, "Yoder, Get your ass out here. You won't want to miss this!" He pulled the covers over his head, resisted, then gave into Josh as he always did, trusting him to spot a winner.

Outside it was still dark. The ground squeaked with each step as he crossed the hundred yards between the house and animal sheds, wrapped in Josh's wool coat that gathered ice, trailing on the ground behind him. The cow was in the largest shed, cleared now of the other animals. Two bulls and a goat lay outside on the frozen ground and he glanced at them with pity, shrugging his shoulders in sympathy as he passed. Pushing open the splintery door, he saw Ruth bent over a small heater, warming her hands. Light from three kerosene lamps gave the shed a ritual glow. She nodded to him, whispered, "it's close," and turned back to the heater.

The cow stood in the center of the shed, moaning quietly and swaying from side to side, her head hanging near the ground. She was the color of soft sandstone, her swollen belly dark and mottled. Occasionally she took a few small steps but mostly stood still, her legs planted firmly in the straw.

Yoder watched from a corner, keeping out of the way and quiet, only nodding at Josh's whispered explanations. He stared in horror as the water sac, an opaque bubble of heavily veined membrane, appeared and receded, signaling each contraction, until it burst and was forced out all at once. Soon after, a hoof appeared, dangling down

93

from the mother, shiny black and hard. The rest of the calf came slowly, taking an hour to inch its way out. When the forelegs cleared, they remained crossed, one hoof placed demurely on top and slightly above the other. Finally, in a quick slippery movement, the shoulders emerged and, lurching slightly, the cow dropped her calf to the ground with an unpleasant thud.

Josh gave a quiet cheer, hugging Ruthie and slapping Yoder on the back. Yoder felt numb. He couldn't take his eyes off the bloody bundle that lay confused in the hay. Making whispered reassurances to the mother, Josh checked the calf for signs of trouble. She repeated his actions, shifting her great weight with effort and began to remove the translucent mucus which clung to the calf's body in strings. The air turned hot and steamy, filled with the sound of her tongue slapping against wet skin. No one spoke above a whisper.

Caught up in the spectacle, they simply stared as the calf rolled onto its side, poking blindly at its mother's belly.

"Don't you dare!" Josh muttered. He jumped up from his seat on a hay bale and rushed over to pull them apart.

"Give me a hand, Yoder."

The cow fought, holding her ground, refusing to be led away. Ruthie stroked the calf's neck, singing under her breath while they tugged at the mother and secured her in a stall. Dodging thrashing hoofs, Josh milked the cow and transferred the steaming liquid to a glass bottle capped with a metal nipple. The calf drank in natural rhythm, its head tilted back on Josh's lap, eyes focused, looking directly into his own.

Moving up close behind Paul, Yoder hissed, "Why'd you do that?"

"You gotta," he said, his eyes on the calf. "Otherwise they bond at this first feeding and it's impossible to separate them."

"So?" Yoder curled his hands inside the fleece lined pockets, stomped his feet for warmth.

"Easy for you to say. So? Ever raise cows, my friend? I tell ya, with our first calf we didn't know any better. Relied on nature to guide us through it. Well, they bonded and it was all very lovable but nothing but trouble from then on. They wanted to feed together, wouldn't go into separate stalls. The mother became incredibly

aggressive. Stepped on my foot and gave me a hell of a bruise. And —
get this — when we sold the mother — now I know this sounds
ridiculous — but both Ruthie and I saw the calf cry."

"What?"

"I swear. So anyway, it's better this way. Separate them before
the attachment is made. Neither one will ever know the difference."

"You sound real sure about that."

"I am," Josh said, pulling the bottle from the calf's mouth.
"Enough."

Within an hour the rest of the animals were fed, milked and
secured in stalls. Walking back to the house, Yoder used his arm to
shield his eyes against the sudden brightness. Josh and Ruth walked
ahead, arms around each other's waist, replaying the entire process in
gestures and giggles. Josh leaned back in Ruthie's embrace and called
over his shoulder, "Comin' in for breakfast?" Yoder shook his head.
He felt no hunger nor any desire to eat and hoped they would leave
him alone.

He remained outside on the small back porch, closing his eyes
and resting in the warming morning sun. Drifting, he thought of the
calf, its head a small copy of its mother's hanging out below the cow's
tail, a grotesque two headed monster waiting for the rest of its body
to be freed. Didn't believe Josh's claim that calf and mother would
feel no connection following the morning's ordeal. Wondered if his
own birth had been as beautiful and mechanical. He knew none of the
details; not the time, nor how much he had weighed, nor the number
of hours his mother had labored. She never spoke of it and he had
never been able to ask.

He still clung to a childhood belief that he had not been born in
any ordinary way. At eleven or twelve he had begun to look at his
parents in a different light — watching and trying to imagine their
coupling. He had thought it sneaky and resented that his own life had
begun without his knowledge or consent. Later, as he grew more and
more distant from his parents, he felt sure that — at the very least, he
was an orphan. To his friends he told an elaborate story about life in
the orphanage, leaving his true origin open to speculation. Privately,
he preferred to believe he had been born on another planet entirely
and dropped mistakenly onto this alien world. Thus he had no real

ties to it, no ancestral connection to the species with whom he had been forced to live.

The door banged shut as Ruth came outside, holding a heaping plate of scrambled eggs, thick bread and a pile of sticky homemade jam which only she seemed able to eat. She sat down on the dry edge of the porch under the slatted wooden roof, glancing at him between bites. He pretended not to notice but watched from behind fluttering eyelids.

"So what did you think of it?" She looked up at him with the smile he always took as a challenge. "You seemed uneasy there at the end."

"It was all right." He closed his eyes and put his head back against the side of the house, not wanting to discuss it with her. He wished she would eat somewhere else. The smell of the food was making him nauseous.

Ruthie's face squeezed into a grimace. "It was all right," she mimicked. "Come on. If you didn't have a stronger reaction, I've been giving you too much credit. Didn't you find it disturbing?"

Opening one eye, he turned slightly to look at her, to see what was behind the question. He had expected a lecture on the wonders of birth.

"Did you?"

"Yes, I did," she said, "at first. It seemed unconscious. Without feeling. Neither seemed aware of the other nor that anything extraordinary had happened. The production of a milking machine, that's all. Made me wonder if I would feel that empty."

"Um." He nodded absently.

She tapped his shoulder with the back of her hand. "What did you really think?"

Eyes closed, he answered. "Mostly how shitty it was that Josh separated them."

"Oh, that. Well, you have to."

"Yeah, yeah, he told me the reasons. I don't know much about animals but that calf knew its mother. You could see it."

"Yoder, they have to be separated. And believe me, it's easier if there's no bond."

"For who? If the birth seemed empty, you're the ones who made it that way." The silence told him he had hit a vulnerable spot. Ruth never left the last word to someone else. When she spoke again it was with a coyness he resented from her.

"You ever thought about having kids, Yoder?"

"I don't think that's the question here. You ever thought about having a kid, Ruth?"

Her face froze and he realized the question was more complicated than he had intended. She seemed to withdraw a moment, as if trying to recall some forgotten name, fingering her hair absently. She tossed her head. "Not unless some miracle happens."

"What do you mean?"

"What do you think? Josh had a vasectomy."

Yoder flinched. "When?"

"Didn't he tell you? Just before he came out here. When he believed the world wasn't any place for a child. Humanitarian reasons, you know, good reasons." When she smirked, she looked coarse and spoiled.

He let out a breath. "How do you feel about it?"

"How do I feel about it?" Ruth cocked an eye at him as if deciding whether to be honest. "I think it's a crime. He has no right to deprive us of his children. He's selfish and impulsive. Part of me hates him for doing it. That answer your question?" She flopped back against the side of the house, holding her plate limply in her hand.

More than ever, he wished she would go away. He didn't want to hear this from her and wondered why Josh had said nothing.

"No right? Who does then? You're making a very important decision for another human being here. Give someone life and you give them death."

"That's ridiculous. Are you that afraid of dying?"

"Nothing to fear in death. It's life you have to think twice about."

"That's not the point, Yoder. I want to give birth."

"Has he been to a doctor? Sometimes they can. . . ."

"Yes, yes. don't you think we've thought of that? It's irreversible. You know Josh — when he has something done, it's done right." She pulled her hair back off her forehead. "I don't know why I'm talking to you about this anyway. Except that you're probably the one who put the idea in his head in the first place."

He held up his hand. "Wait. I didn't ever know about it 'til just now."

"Oh, all right. It's not your concern." She sighed heavily, looking over at him with a hint of amusement. "See, you're not the only one with problems."

"Who ever said I was?"

"Oh, it's your attitude. 'Nobody understands me.' 'Nobody loves me.' It gets tiresome, really."

Laughing, he shook his head, amazed that she had finally admitted what he'd always known. Her dislike had been apparent from the moment he knocked on their door. "You should have said something before."

She rubbed her eyes in exaggerated circles. "Look, it's just that I'm tired of hearing about how you've been misunderstood all of your life. Like you're the only one who ever felt that way."

He looked over at her wearily. "Listen, Ruthie, everyone understands. They just don't know what to do about it. Isn't that right?" He paused, considering her. The sun was lighting up her face, showing lines, making her look older than usual. "You understand why I'm here and so do I but that doesn't answer your question. . . . How long am I staying? You might get stuck with me forever, like some kind of disabled in-law, right Ruthie? You think I should go stay with my folks or something until I get it together, don't you? Well, I'll tell you something, there's a lot less between me and them then there is between you and I."

"No one asked you to leave." She said the words flatly, but studied him with a hint of alarm.

"No? There's been too much snow to work on the house for three days now. I'm lousy with the animals. I'm not earning my keep around here. But I don't know any better than you where the hell I'm going to go."

"Goddamn it, Yoder. Cut it out. Josh likes having you here and that's that."

They were both shouting, suddenly disrespectful of the country silence. He held her eyes until she looked away. "Maybe I believe you." Dropping his head into his hands, he spoke quietly and with difficulty. "Look, this isn't the place for me. I know that. But I honestly don't physically know where to go from here."

Something clicked in the back of his neck, like a shell snapping into its chamber. He sprang off the porch, his face contorted and red, prepared to kill or cry. Bending down, he scratched a handful of small stones from the frozen ground and threw them with force at the chicken coop, rattling the wire mesh. The flurry of squawks brought a smile to his face and he threw another handful.

"I'd just like to know what I'm supposed to do now. I'm twenty-nine years old and I don't have anything. And I know it's my fault — probably it's my own fault. Get a job. I should get a job." He waved his arm at her. "Christ, you know all about that. What job could I do without feeling like puking all the time? And I don't feel misunderstood. I don't care about being understood." With this he swung his leg around, kicking the porch post full force, absorbing the pain and speaking directly to Ruth. "Don't get me wrong. I like being here but I don't belong here. I got put here and I'm supposed to hang around until someday I die. What kind of arrangement is that? Now you tell me?"

He shook his fist at her, his whole arm trembling. Throwing his head back, he stumbled, shouting MOTHERFUCKERS so loud that Ruth glanced quickly around for opening doors and disapproving faces. When she turned back, he was seated on the porch step, head buried in his knees. Josh's woolen coat fell around him, hiding his body. She sat down beside him and put her arm around his small shoulders. He flinched, pulled away and burrowed down into the warmth of his knees, eyes clenched against the light. Pressing hard into the darkness, he began to swim, tried to drown.

Replaying the morning like a movie flickering, his voice echoed loud in his ears. MOTHERFUCKERS. How many had heard? Memories surfaced in no order, fragmented like the stray melodies which played when his mind was at rest. Vision of a woman he had seen days before in town, streaming by, red hair flying; the wine, had he remembered to hide it?; the calf's brown eyes looking up at Josh with the full trust of a child; worry about a lump on the inside of his leg that had appeared the week before.

The crying was outside him, a delayed reaction to frustrations long past. Ruthie's persistent arm around his shoulders was no comfort — he wanted her gone. He wanted them all gone. No, no it was not that. He was the one who needed to disappear in a puff of smoke. He began to notice that her arm tightened in rhythm with his sobbing. He caught himself leaning toward her, wanting to crawl inside to hide.

"Where's Josh?" he asked, his head still buried.

"He's gone to Bangor to pick up some lumber. He said to tell you he'd be back tonight."

At least that was something. Josh was not inside listening to him cry. Yet he could not face Ruthie alone for the rest of the day. Not now. He'd been hiding from her all these weeks, careful not to reveal anything important. She had the power to change Josh's feelings. That was the worst of it. That Josh trusted someone else more. Rocking slowly, he waited for answers to surface, then started to speak without thinking, talking to his knees.

"When I was eighteen, I almost got married. She was skinny, with long legs and curly brown hair, two years younger than me and always in trouble. We started getting into trouble together, setting off firecrackers in mailboxes, spray-painting stuff on the cop house, stealing bigger and bigger things. She was great at shoplifting. Stole a pair of skis right off the floor of our biggest store. Just walked in and walked out with them. We never even used 'em, we couldn't ski but it was the idea of it.

"I was the one who wanted to get married; that seems impossible now. I wanted to hold on to her. I had a job at a cannery, it was all planned out. I was going to work, save money and then we were going to take off, this was back in the days when everything was possible. She loved to travel. Had this postcard collection that she liked to look at and plan trips to see the things on the cards. She said it didn't make sense to live on earth and not see it all, that that was the least a person could do." He blew his nose into the sleeve of Josh's coat. He could feel Ruthie leaning closer, listening.

"Anyway, I don't know why she left, nothing happened. Hell, she wasn't old enough to go very far away, I thought. I tried to find her but her parents swore they didn't know where she was. A couple of fucking liars, that's what they were. And here's the thing. Since then, I've been in love *fifty* times and every time I've been really happy. But no one ever loves me back for more than a little while. Not like she did."

He raised his head, brushing tears from his cheeks, looking red-eyed at Ruthie. "I'll tell you what it's like," he said. "It's like a winter day here when the sun has gone behind a cloud. You shiver, adjusting to the loss and the dullness of the light. Then suddenly, it begins to come on strong again, stronger by the second. You hold your breath, waiting to see how hot it will burn, how bright it will be. It changes everything, lengthens the shadows, makes it all more intense, the trees, water, cars, grass, the backs of ducks, your blue jeans, the hairs on your arm. And then just when you're the warmest, it goes, leaving slowly like it came, sucking the light away until you're more chilled than you ever have been, hugging yourself to shake off the cold." He kicked the mud back against the step with his heel. "It's the one thing I know. I know she loved me but I don't know why she left."

Ruth lowered her eyes. She could think of no words to say and wished Josh were inside to walk with him, to take him away. Standing up, brushing off her pants, she mumbled. "I don't know, Yoder. I don't know," and crossed in front of him to reach a bucket of chicken feed hanging from a nail on the side of the porch. She ran her hands through the grains and seeds, her anger and sympathy for him growing. Setting the bucket down she stepped over to the door.

"That happens, Yoder. To all of us." There was an impatient edge to her voice. "But that was 11 years ago. I hope you aren't going to say from that day on life lost all meaning, because then, well, then you're in worse shape than I thought." She shook her head slowly, a frown imbedded in her forehead. She reached out her hand but he refused it and she went inside, closing the door very softly behind her.

"I only told you that because it came to mind," he shouted after her. "Damn." He unbuttoned Josh's coat and dropped it to the ground. Shaking back his hair, he looked around at the landscape of chicken coops, dead cars and the patchy hills rising and falling toward the ocean. The morning deserved to be over though by the sun and he knew it could be no more than 10 o'clock. The calf was four hours old. He began to walk toward the sheds.

The sun had melted the top layer of icy snow and the ground

gave slightly under his feet. He bent his head to enter the shed where the new calf and its mother stood, separated by a stall wall. It was dark and it took a few minutes for his eyes to adjust. Its large eyes stared patiently into the darkness. He approached it apprehensively and, when it seemed not to mind his presence, sat down beside it. He stroked the calf's head in slow motions, as the mother, bending her head around the partition, watched.

The Lip Collector

William Meissner

H E WANTS TO OWN all the lips in the world so he'll never be alone. With a sharpened stare, he cuts off the lips of everyone he meets. Then he keeps them in a wooden box at the foot of his bed. He even cuts off his own lips, leaving a strange silent blur below his nose.

At first, he and the lips are friends; all day they talk to him, and at night their songs light up around him like angels as he falls asleep.

But the lips begin to whisper to themselves. He knows this, and he fears they are falling in love with each other. So he ties each pair shut with wire.

The next morning the lips are gone. Even his own lips had crawled out of the box like moist red worms, holding their breath so they wouldn't wake him.

He talks to no one now. He spends his days looking for the lips: in old letter boxes, behind the radio, between sticking pages of photo albums. He knows they're still somewhere in his house — some nights they wake him with their selfish passion, all of them puckering against one another in one huge, loud kiss.

The Field

Lawrence Sutin

D RIVING TO THE country lakehouse Jeff and Terri had rented, I
found that listening to the radio made me tired. The music
touched off memories to which I could no longer respond: useless,
persistent hermits in the head. I tried to wash them away, to
anticipate the placid lake setting to come. When I saw the exit sign
for Ridge Lane I sighed so loudly I made myself laugh. Ridge Lane
was covered by a thick spillage of gravel on which my tires made
fierce chewing noises. I skidded badly but couldn't convince myself to
slow down, being so close. It was a narrow road: branches raked my
car and snapped in the open windows. To the left, through the gaps
in the darkly huddled pines, poplars and elms, I could see the lake:
blue vitriol boiling in sunlight.

Jeff had said that I would recognize their house by seeing them
outside it drinking. Terri, his wife, I had met twice before, small
glances in the midst of larger conversations. Jeff assured me that she
was flourishing in their new setting and would welcome my company
for the weekend; their goal of time apart for themselves had been
reached and then surpassed. I brought along a sack of groceries, nice
treats: olives, pickles, potato salad, ice cream, burgundy wine. I
imagined myself seated beside the lake, staring out over it, until the
smallest ripples at its center seemed to reach me at once.

There he was, barechested and brown, the bulging ridge of black
curly hair topping his head like a rooster's comb. When I pulled
alongside him he spread his arms and smiled so fully I thought the
shoulder muscles had to be involved somhow.

"Well, you made it! You and the old heap made it!" He gave the
door a little kick.

My car was streaked with rust and needed maintenance badly.
My job made me too tired to face small, cumulative necessities, and
when they finally fell on me I was usually frantic. I reassured myself
by noticing how many others behaved this way. But Jeff wasn't one of
those. Inside himself were reasons for everything as he needed them:
a fuel substance, like adrenalin, but unrelated to standard excitements
and dangers.

He handed me a beer. I pointed at my grocery sack, wanting him to know that I didn't intend to sponge for two days, but he waved off my gesture and jumped onto the roof of my car, swinging his legs. It was heavy, humid air, woolly feeling. The cold beer can almost slipped from between my fingers. I found a beach chair to sit down in, groggy from the drive. Jeff was by my side, hand on my shoulder, solicitous already, I felt a little ashamed.

"You look as though you've lived in a file cabinet all your life. Too much time in the office, Henry. Am I right?"

"I'll be o.k. I just have to learn how to move my body again. I've forgotten how to do everything except sit."

"But you feel like you want some fast action, right? Jesus, I hope so."

"Yeah, I'm sure I do."

"Great. Just look over there, buddy." Jeff picked up a stone from the driveway and threw it hard in a high arc. It landed in the midst of a broad green field shaped like a horse's back. The lake was just below where the neck would continue to rise on a horse. Scattered poplars edged the field's sides. "I mowed the whole damn thing yesterday. Took me four hours. There's no place in the city as good for frisbee playing. We can go outright nuts."

"Oh yeah."

"God I've been looking forward to this. You're the only one who can keep up with me when I get truly crazy. Better give you a little time to unwind, though. You're not done with that beer? You know how much booze we've got out here? I got a deal on some Mexican brew. Three cases, wholesale prices. I'll get you some. That domestic stuff is o.k. for casual sipping, though. Gets you in the mood to really drink. You didn't bring any work out here with you, did you?" He was bracing on one foot and then the other, hands cupping the edges of his waist. I had sweat on my eyelids already.

"Terri!" he yelled. "Jeeze," he said, turning back to me, "she told me this morning she was looking forward to talking to anybody who wasn't me. That's what happens when you live isolated in paradise — you find out that love is a drug and you need to be careful with the dosages. We've made ourselves so hyper trying to trust and please each other that weird kinky types like you could start to look real interesting. You watch yourself, though, because my old lady can be a mean son of a bitch, not patient like me. So when she smiles at you you smile back, o.k.?"

I *was* starting to smile. Jeff was good at sensing things and taking over. I had a brief sense of envy toward Terri for being married to him and having him smooth out her moods so often. Jeff could let you risk being careless. I watched her emerge from the house holding a tall glass. She was doing a kind of slithery dance, wearing a black string bikini that showed what a clean, firm shape she had. Jeff, on the way in for my beer, slapped her on the ass and the sound was like a water balloon breaking. She kicked at him and he grabbed her leg, both of them giggling. They both balanced their drinks and it struck me that the reason they were feeling good while I wasn't was because they were drunk and I wasn't even trying to be. Terri fell into the wicker chaise lounge across from me. Her eyes were focusing at the tip of her nose; the last time I had seen her she was wearing glasses. I was relieved not to be particularly attracted to her, though she was attractive. Her blond hair was cut short to emphasize her ears, delicate ones, like ivy leaves. She was talking while holding the edge of the drink on her lower lip.

"I feel as though I should know you by now. Jeff has told me about everything you two used to do, minus a few episodes, I'm sure, but anyway, it's good you could get out here."

"Thank you for having me."

"Oh come on! Don't apologize. It's not even close to being a minor imposition. This house is a steal. The rent is peanuts and it's bigger than we need. Actually it's all pretty decadent. Neither of us wants to work again in the fall. Know what? I'm going to have Jeff support me. A kept woman. Still, out here by myself all winter I'd probably start humping the mailman. Actually we can't stay out here anyway. Both of us are born and bred for city life, damn it. This whole summer is a one-time splurge."

"I should do the same thing."

"You should! I don't know if any of the other houses are available, but I'll ask tonight. Our landlords, the Swensons, are also our next door neighbors — they're coming by for drinks. We get along with them fine. I think living by this lake mellows people out. That and money. They own nearly all the houses along here except that red one across the field. The Swensons are set for life. Real estate's crazy money, that's why Jeffrey wants to get into it. Don't you think he can wheel and deal?" She looked up.

"For sure he can."

"Damn right," Jeff said from behind me. "Isn't that beer of yours gone? Chug it. Chug it right now." I did. "Now drink this. You've got three minutes." It was a dark bottle with a gaudy, gold-crowned bull on the label.

"I still think beer tastes like mule piss," Terri said.

"Only not as rich, right?"

"Shut up, Jeffrey. God it's way too early for us all to be drunk. Or isn't Henry drunk?"

"Henry, are you drunk?"

"Working on it."

"Don't use that word this weekend, pal. You know what we named this place? Poopout Palace. No one lifts a finger here 'til October, unless it's to summon our butler, Rudolfo. Where is Rudolfo anyhow?"

"Took the day off again."

"The day! He hasn't showed his face since we got here. That old packrat must be holed up somewhere waiting for an advance."

I was staring at them both.

"Rudolfo doesn't really exist, Henry," Terri said pityingly.

"I know," I said. But I hadn't. My face went red. I was boring two drunks. I chugged the Mexican beer too. "Is there more? I've got to stop feeling so lame."

"Kitchen. You'll find it." Jeff gave me his best smile. "Stop being so nervous. In an hour you'll be out of it as we are." He lifted Terri's legs, sat down beneath them and dropped them back onto his lap. She wiggled them across his thighs. "Someone's waiting for you in the bedroom, Henry. Our maid. I don't think Terri's met her."

"It's only Rudolfo in drag, dearest. Or did you *want* to be fooled?"

Jeff leaned to kiss one of her ivy ears.

On top of the refrigerator was a bottle of tequila. I took a long tug, licking my sweaty wrist for salt, remembering that beer and tequila didn't go together too badly. It was too long a tug, though: the

insides of my cheeks crawled. I cut myself a piece of cheese and took a
beer. Just as I was finishing chewing Jeff came in with my grocery
bag. I started blushing again for having filched the cheese.

"Fuck, are you drunk yet?"

"Damn near almost."

"Finish up and then let's play some frisbee. We need music." He
set the bag on the table. While I unpacked it, he called out album
names from the living room until I agreed on one. When it began I
couldn't hear it clearly and asked him why.

"Because the speakers are pointing out the windows. Let's get
down there onto that field."

"Can you do that?"

"Why the hell not? This is the country."

"Great!"

We were both excited. I had made it safely into drunkenness. We
ran outside past Terri who gave us a little wave and a thin smile. As
her features were pinched to begin with, the smile forced her face
into a squinting, derisive mask. I remembered her fierce explanation
to me about Rudolfo and felt uncomfortable about spending the
weekend near her. She seemed too determined to have a good time,
or certain that she wouldn't.

Jeff threw the frisbees out over the field before we got there.
They hung, swooped and fell, fluttering. He ran for them. We had
lost touch for a few years. Jeff had moved away, found a wife, come
back. We were still close. I felt that, watching him. But I was worried
we were stuck being friends in a younger way. That wasn't so bad,
with the music. I was still having trouble getting out of the office. Jeff
was perfect for helping me do that.

We both took off our shirts. I was covered with sweat right off.
Jeff glided right along, jumping and diving even more than he had to.
At first we shouted back and forth but that stopped. There were no
jokes left in us; we just wanted to run and throw. It was perfect
terrain, a large soft bowl with a horizon of iridescent lakeshore and
poplars with blinking leaves. When my body grew used to the effort
involved I changed gears completely and grew jumpy and eager like
Jeff, hopping up and down waiting for his tosses. We threw faster
and harder, deliberately making the other run the maximum

possible. I proudly curved one far out over the lake and back to him; he caught it on the run, whirled, screamed some kind of war cry, and sent a softly spinning, gliding throw over my head. Chasing it I saw a woman approching us from the red house on the opposite side of the field. In her yard a large dog was chained to a tree. I couldn't remember seeing it there before.

Her face, wide from forehead to ears, concluded in a soft, rounded chin, like a pear. Her cheeks were so full they seemed swollen, like freshly risen biscuits; but her skin was pale. Her long, brown hair was bound up in a loose bun, with strands escaping and wavering in the air. As she walked she stared at the ground, a deliberate pose, I thought, to avoid looking at me. I said hello and she nodded but moved on quickly. Her nod showed me how round and deepset dark her eyes were. She reminded me of a raccoon. I threw the frisbee over her departing head back to Jeff. He caught it and waited, then walked toward her, meeting her midway. As they spoke the familiar gestures began to explode from his body: waving arms, tossing head, hair pulling (his own). She only swayed slightly, stiff-legged. Behind her back I could see her wringing her hands. In a few minutes it was over. She walked carefully past me again, back to her yard where she stood beside the chained dog and petted it. I motioned for the frisbee. Jeff bit into it and then stamped on the ground. When I drew near him he was already talking to himself and only increased his volume.

"I just can't believe it. I mowed this whole damn field yesterday. She had to hear the noise. And now this."

"What?"

"She's kicked us off. We're through. Private property. No trespassing."

"It's her field?"

"The bitch."

"I don't understand. Haven't you ever talked to her about using it?"

"There was no reason to. The Swensons told me everyone used it for softball and picnics for years. But that crazy lady is new here this summer. It's her uncle who owns the house and property, and she wants us off We're bothering her. She says she's here to rest. The music is especially horrible for her."

"Maybe she's afraid one of us will slip and fall and sue her for injuries."

"Oh come on, Henry. I'd rather believe she was vicious than paranoid."

"She seemed really sad."

"She *is*. She's a mental basket case. She tries to freeze her face while she's talking to you. I think she's really scared of us. She even threatened to call the cops. Come on, let's get off this holy ground of hers."

"Are we going to turn down the music?"

"Never."

I must have looked startled, because he toned down and tried to convince me. "When she first asked me to leave I thought she might just be feeling cranky, so I took it slow. I asked did she see me mow the lawn. She said no, she was out all yesterday, which is bullshit, since I saw that car of hers in the driveway the whole time I was out there. So then I said her uncle always let people use the field. 'He's crazy,' she said. Imagine her calling her uncle crazy to a complete stranger. But I was still holding everything in. I asked if she didn't want to try to be good neighbors, since we're out here in paradise together. She says no flat out. So I told her, that's it, I'm through talking. Talking to a wall."

"She seems strange."

"No kidding."

Terri had watched the whole thing. She was laughing when we got back.

"O.K., baby," Jeff told her. "Strategy time." We sat in the living room and drank more of the Mexican beer. Jeff rolled three joints and we smoked them in a row. It was more than we needed or wanted and we all stopped trying to hold our inhalations. Smoke streamed out of Jeff's nostrils as he shook his head. The combined effect of everything — heat, beer and dope, listening to the lake lapping against the shoreline — made me want to sleep. Terri asked if I was hungry. I smiled and stretched out on the carpet. "Maybe we can swim in a bit," I said, trying to let her know that I would feel active later.

"You look like a tabby cat," Terri said. "Watch out. Our carpet sheds lint."

"I've found my plan of action." Jeff announced., "Dope puts me into states of pure concentration. Most people don't use it that way. Can you see her out there?" Through the window facing across the field we could. The woman, the dog next to her, stood in the backyard facing the field.

"What kind of dog is that?" I asked.

"An akita," Terri said. She saw it didn't register. "A spitz, pointy ears, an attack dog."

Then she really is crazy!" But then I was sorry I said that.

Jeff belched gently, "You are starting to catch on. Good thing she didn't come after us with it."

"An attack dog?"

"I don't know if Terri's right about that. She could be. I've got a plan. Just harassment, for now. When the Swensons come over tonight we'll talk major protest."

"Turn up the music?"

"More subtle."

I rolled my eyes, wanting out. Jeff took his camera from the top of the bookshelf. A telephoto lens sprouted from its center.

"Pictures!" Terri piped. "Is there film in it?"

"No. It doesn't matter." Jeff left the room. Terri and I went to the window. He emerged from below us, walked to the edge of the field, knelt, then swung the camera, prodding it toward the woman and the dog, focusing carefully between feigned shots. He would be seeing them clearly through the telephoto lens. They did not move at first. Then she must have startled, for we saw her turn and go, leading the dog into the house.

He returned, smiling and staring at us.

"All's well, thank you," he said, sitting down and beginning to roll another joint. "This is turning into a Sufi fable. There's a book of those on the shelf there. They're amazing. Thank God for dope. It evens things out. The intricacies begin to flow. You should have seen her face! I was watching the muscles twitching in her cheeks. Her face was like water just before it boils. She knew what I was doing — or she thought she did! It was beautiful."

"Did you get a look at the dog?" I asked. Jeff exhaled the dope and nodded.

"Did the dog look angry?" Terri asked, laughing.

"Hey, the dog wants three copies of any of the photos that come out well. It's great."

I was at the window; her house could have contained three bedrooms. "Is she living there completely alone?"

"Ease up, Henry. Here, finish this yourself." Jeff handed me the joint. "A good smoke means a good appetite, and it's time to eat. Let's cook up a feast."

I did feel hungry as soon as he said that. The dope made me fasten onto his suggestions. I regretted not looking at the woman and the dog through the lens myself; it might have subdued them inside me.

"Would you have a book with a picture of an akita in it?"

They laughed. I started to laugh too. Jeff was gasping: "Henry, marry her. I mean it. You do that, she'll let us use the field for sure. I think you two would understand each other."

I thought he might not be so far wrong. It was hard to celebrate with them over the camera ploy because I could sense how frightening it might be to have hostile neighbors photograph you from a distance. Images could be used for ridicule. You could never be sure what you accidentally looked like at any particular moment. Snapshots of myself showed me every which way, usually badly. A fear of being observed often struck me when I felt sad or nervous, such as just after work, when the bars closest to my office were impossible to enter. The akita faded in my mind a bit, or justified itself. She was being a bitch about the field but otherwise I was starting to sympathize with her. Jeff could have asked her permission directly rather than rely on the Swensons' say so. My head was full of debates.

Cooking outside was a pleasure. We grilled chicken and burgers, which allowed for a long, restful wait. Meanwhile we ate all my pickles and olives and salad and continued, after some iced tea, to go at the Mexican beer. Just as we were finishing the Swensons came by with a bottle of dark rum. Having my stomach full helped me stay calm despite the liquor. Tom Swenson wore green checkered pants and a black golf shirt with his initials on the pocket. He had a deep tan and looked over fifty, full of sly, bright memories. His hair was tinted to move it over into a kind of silver. He shook the bottle of dark rum at us like a marimba and laughed, then went inside to mix drinks. Jill Swenson, fine time lines edging her chin, sat in a one-piece pink swimsuit from which her body was escaping at the edges. She looked first at Terri and then at me and said, "Your friend's adapted to lake life pretty quickly."

I asked: "Do I look so drunk?"

"Don't be upset, kiddo. Everyone looks like what they are. I look my age, don't I?"

"How old are you?" I asked very loud.

"Henry's loaded," Jeff said. "Right, Henry?"

"Righto," I answered, smiling.

When Tom returned Jeff told the Swensons about the incident on the field. Both of them became indignant. Tom had concocted an excellent pitcher of some sort of rum drink and I relaxed so much I began to laugh at Jeff's story myself and added on details of my own about how she walked as though she were afraid her ass would come unglued. Jill was on my side now, laughing and petting my shoulder.

"I remember her from when she used to come out to visit her uncle," Tom said. "We invited them over for barbeque pretty often. Wayne Lockeridge, that was her uncle's name, didn't have any kids of his own. His wife died young. He finally remarried and moved away, but he held onto the house, though I offered to buy him out. Anyway, the girl was always shy. I can't remember her damn name, though."

"No one ever used it," Jill told him. "Wayne gave her a nickname — Dilly."

"That's right! That's right! Dilly!" He saw us all giggling and broke down too. "You know, that name really figures, now that I think about it. Wayne sort of treated her like a pet he used to cheer himself up. He would talk and play with her for a while and then get bored. It took him a while to figure out how to be single again. Once he did though, he had women out here all the time, a real parade. I don't think Dilly much cared for any of them. She wandered around by herself a lot."

"Maybe Dilly had a crush on Wayne," I said.

"That's possible," Jill agreed. "Wayne had a nice ass."

"She was a lovely kid," Tom continued. "She didn't play much with the other boys and girls. The couple times I met her parents they sat facing opposite directions and smoking down a pack apiece. They had money."

"Lots." Jill said. "Dilly used to have her own horse. It grazed and shat all over that damn field. Then they sold it. She didn't want to ride it. She'd rather play with that akita, I guess. I don't think she's been back out here for a couple of years. But with Wayne gone the house is really hers." She leaned back. I could smell her cocoanut tanning oil in the shifting, cooling air. With my swirling rum high I could see us all floating in a vast tropical drink, stirred by a lazy finger of wind.

"What that girl needs is fucking," Jill decided, pinching my thigh. Jeff pointed at me approvingly and I said, eager to keep pleasing, "Sure, I'll take her on." I was enjoying the vague sense of acknowledged desire that most kinds of kidding about sex provides. As for Dilly in particular, without seriously conceiving anything, I could feel how flattering it would be to arouse her, and how potentially shocking. Who knew what she wanted? It was hard to imagine her as good or even playful in bed.

The sun sank in the mesh of trees across the lake. It looked like an irritated eye trying to open, and then it closed. The Swensons said good night and we gathered up the paper plates and empty cans and bottles and threw them away.

Inside, Terri took a shower and Jeff heated up water for coffee. I decided to take a walk along the narrow beach which the Swensons had assured me belonged to them. More stars showed here than in the city. A slight mist, just enough to make me want to rub my eyes, coated the bristling reeds and cattails growing from the edge of the lake like patches of hair. Frogs croaked from within them. Much of the beach was actually closer to marsh. There were several dead fish along the shoreline, one or two phosphorescent. Jeff had mentioned that a large number were dying and no one knew why. I watched the moonlight on the lake: the creamy patches stretched and shattered in the rising tide. I sat on an old log half-consumed by a previous bonfire. It must have been kindled at one of those long ago summertime picnics the Swensons spoke of so lovingly during drinks, the ones Dilly avoided. So many people had come that the field had been covered with grills, blankets and beer kegs.

What wind there was passed over me, sighing through the leaves. I thought that I could fall asleep easily, still watching everything, the stars, the swaying trees, the lace edge of water coming nearly to my feet. A small noise, barely there, began to repeat itself: footsteps. I didn't know from which direction but then I spotted her, walking with the akita on a leash. She had to be surprised by me too, unless she had been spying on my movements as we had seemed to spy on hers. I saw her stiffen — the akita pulled her for a few steps. Then she recovered, and it strained on the leash and sniffed.

"Hello," I said for the second time that day. She was still fifteen feet away, but because of the akita that seemed natural and even courteous. I was afraid but also thinking that it wasn't her fault. The trees kept the moonlight from reaching her. I could see the shapes and tones of a woman and a dog but none of the features of either. When she spoke to me the voice arrived separately.

"Are you here visiting them?"

"Yes."

"Why did your friend take the pictures?"

"I don't know." I tried to show her, by an exaggerated shrug, that I honestly didn't. She kicked the sand with her foot and wrapped the leash once around her wrist. The akita's head jerked up but it didn't bark.

"I would like that roll of film. I'll pay its retail cost."

"Why? That's silly. There's nothing on it but harmless snapshots. They're probably out of focus."

"Let your friend know that I'll pay him."

Jeff would probably set an exorbitant price, I thought. But there was no real roll of film. I couldn't explain to her what had happened. Dilly wouldn't sympathize with people who were drunk and drugged and tried to act funny. I tried to cut it short and not act that way myself. I only wanted to tell her something that would allow her to forget it.

"Don't worry. He won't even develop it. He doesn't care anymore. I'll steal it from him if he does try to. It was only a stunt to make you nervous."

"You people really are evil, aren't you."

"I mean it. Believe me. Those pictures will never exist."

"Tell him I'll pay. Can you hold that in your head? Or are you too drunk on your ass? How can you stand being away from your music? Aren't there too many exciting things going on for you to be alone out here? Maybe you can pull some more stunts."

"There wasn't even a roll of film inside the camera." It was too late, even assuming a confession would have worked to begin with. I threw it out like a last penny into the well, just to hear the sound it would make.

"There wasn't even a camera, was there? And no one really owns any land here except the Swensons, do they? Isn't this just their party?"

"Look, I barely know them."

"You barely know anything. Isn't that right? I'll bet it is."

The wind and waves were filling my ears. She turned away, yanking the dog, then leaned back over her shoulder. I noticed that her hair was no longer in a bun but swept over her eyes.

"Just tell him I'll pay."

On the way back I almost decided not to tell Jeff and Terri about the meeting. It might encourage more tricks, given Dilly's obvious vulnerability. But then I thought that they ought to know how anxious she really was. Jeff could apologize, even hand her a dummy roll of film. But her obsession would lead her to develop it, leading to further outrage and anguish.

When I did tell them Jeff reacted somberly, shaking his head as though he was conducting a test of some inner sense of things. Terri made a toast in the direction of the window overlooking the field, then splashed her wine into the sink.

"Boys, I'm going to sleep."

Jeff pointed me to the spare bedroom and followed her.

We woke up very late, but in near unison, creeping floor noises reaching me as one of them made their first trip to the bathroom . I took charge of making the coffee. We read the Sunday paper sections. I was surprised to learn that it was delivered to their doorstep. It made it all seem less remote.

It was hot and humid again, with tangled cottonball clouds. Swimming in the lake wasn't refreshing: we felt like ingredients in a soup. Back on the lawn (the beach itself had a hypnotic fish smell) we drank more of the wholesale Mexican beer. That reminded me of Dilly's willingness to pay retail, and I mentioned that, as I had forgotten it in the cautious mood of last night's telling. They were too hot and lazy to laugh, but Jeff was struck by it, as I was. He closed his eyes, grinning, then opened them again.

"We're just sitting here getting old, Henry. How about a little more frisbee?"

"On the field?"

"Where else?"

"We can't." If we played again she would think we were confident of being able to blackmail her. I remembered now that I also hadn't told them about being willing to steal the film.

"Sure we can. The Swensons told me to go ahead."

"I want to play but I don't think so. She'll call the cops."

"Let her. Tom Swenson explained to me all about adverse possession. Since everyone's played on the land for years, we can claim it as a legal right. The cops don't care anyhow. They'll probably tell her to calm down."

"No."

"Maybe they'll bring a tranquilizer gun for the dog, Henry," Terri said. That was old; I wasn't afraid of the dog anymore.

"O.K., Henry, look," said Jeff. "You stand on the driveway. I'll go into the field. You throw to me out there. How's that? Oh come on."

"Fine," I said.

We played. Terri went inside to sleep some more. I didn't put much into my throws, since I wanted Jeff to tire of it as soon as possible. Prior to starting we had smoked a joint together; it hadn't done much except make me watchful. I expected a police car. Instead, after a few minutes, the akita bounded out after Jeff. It moved heavily and looked old. Jeff saw it and sprinted for a tree on our side of the field. He pulled himself up onto the first thick limb, having beaten the akita by several seconds. It stopped, puffing, and stared up at him, though I was nearby and perfect bait. I could finally examine it up close: too fat but still strong, heavy double coat of fur, flat head, short muzzle, erect pink ears, a feathered tail curving over its back. I didn't know what to do.

"Get Terri," Jeff yelled to me. "She loves dogs." He dangled a broken branch at the akita's snout. When it reached up to grab it he batted its head. "Here pooch! Here killer! Hey Henry, this dog has shit for brains, you know?" I started to leave but stopped. Dilly had walked out onto the field holding a pistol. When she whistled the dog returned to her on the run — faster than it had chased Jeff. And Jeff was looking at the ground, his hand on his head, astonished or oblivious, I didn't know which. I ran to get Terri. I thought that was what he wanted.

She woke very slowly, climbing out of her sleep. I had to shake her hard. She was dressed in her bikini and damp all over, smelling of strawberry essence. There was a vial of that, along with bottles of sleeping pills, on the dresser. I explained as fast as I could and what she said was, "What are you doing talking to me?" She ran to the bedroom closet and pulled out a rifle in a tan leather case she unzipped with a tearing motion. Then, after more searching, she came up with a box of bullets. I watched her jam a shell as thick as a finger into the chamber.

"You guys own a gun?"

"Call the police, will you? Jeff shoots ducks that hang out on the lake. We eat them. Now shut up."

I followed her out. I thought it was my duty, even before calling the police. We heard a shot just as we rounded the house and came into view. Jeff dropped down to the ground. The akita went over to him. Dilly threw the pistol away and started to curl up, shoulders hunched and forward, hands wrapped over her mouth. Jeff rose up on one knee and then, as if he couldn't hear or see anything, tipped over.

Dilly took small steps forward and screamed: "It was a warning shot! It was a warning shot!" She looked at his stiff, sidewards face and started to beg: "Did you try to hurt my dog? Was that it?"

Terri levelled the rifle and charged her. The way I am made, no matter what I see, my surprise never lasts more than a second. I did not shout before Terri reached Dilly, and Dilly never looked up. She was bending over and talking to him, asking over and over what it was he had wanted from her. Terri knelt down beside her and peered at her husband's face, hunting for a reaction, then shook him hard, making his head slap loosely from shoulder to shoulder like a buoy. Dilly reached out a hand to make her stop. When she was touched Terri stood up in a jerk, backpedaled a few steps and shot her dead, aiming down the rifle until the echo faded. Then she turned to me. I ran

A Treasure

Judith Serin

Dear Julie,

I've purchased a young man. It was purely on impulse. You know I usually don't go in for that kind of extravagance. Before this, I never understood why a woman would want one.

I saw him in a shop window a couple of weeks ago. The weather had just turned to fall, snapped into it overnight. You know how these seasonal changes stir you up, arouse old feelings of longing from a time when you still believed that your life was susceptible to sudden change, to magical solutions? So I was walking more slowly than usual, dawdling, waiting for some shape to emerge from the ambiguous gray of this city's streets, structures, and sky. I noticed him in one of those awful, glittering window displays, a miracle of mirrors and fake snow. He was seated in an elaborate papier-mache sled, swan-shaped and drawn by four impossibly delicate horses. He leaned his elbows on its rococo wing, his chin in his hands, a childlike gesture. He had a watchfulness which matched my own. A placard in the corner of the window announced "SALE".

I thought only my curiosity was aroused. I called to a salesman lounging in the doorway, "How come he's on sale? Is he sick?"

"Oh no," the fellow replied in a tone that managed to be both obsequious and friendly. "He's last season's model. We're making room for the new look."

"Why didn't anyone buy him?"

"Not goodlooking, I guess," the salesman shrugged.

Not goodlooking! I turned toward the boy, who looked back at me with a suspicion of interest. My longing crystallized. He was lovely, perfect, a treasure. Oh not all blond and cold and muscular like those little animals sopranos parade at parties. He was round faced and brown eyed and held himself with an unselfconscious grace. His skin was smooth, his features rounded like his face. And the hair, the perfect short black curls, like a poodle, like a child's stuffed toy.

The salesman sensed my shift. "I can give him to you for 10% off. He's in very good condition."

"Ten percent!" I knew I must bargain coldly hide my newborn

desire. "Last season's look — I can't go anywhere with him. I'd only buy him out of charity."

In brief, I argued the salesman down to half price, while the boy flushed. Poor thing, I thought, this hurts his pride. I'll console him when we get home. He'll cry and I'll hold him. I'll be his savior, his life.

Well Julie, he didn't cry. I took him to the bedroom, and he curled up and went to sleep. I sat there watching him. He wheezed a little, probably has allergies. When I reached to touch his hair, he turned his head away.

He isn't trained. I thought they were taught what to do, but he obviously doesn't know a thing. And he doesn't speak the language. When I talk to him, he shakes his head politely. I've heard him murmuring to the cats in some undefinable tongue. I tried to teach him my name, hoping he would reveal his in return. I sat him down on the blue couch and settled next to him. "Carla," I enunciated, pointing at myself, "Car-la." He watched courteously. He didn't repeat after me or offer any word in his own language. I said, "Carla," poking my chest, at least twenty times. My strained smile made the corners of my mouth ache. When my hands fell into my lap in defeat, he sprang up and returned to the bedroom, where he finished sketching the fish in my aquarium. The drawings are accurate and elegant.

Julie, I can hear your indignant voice, "It's an outrage. Bring him back. Haul that unscrupulous salesman into court . . ." But I can't. I feel sheepish writing this, but I'm in love with him. I can't think of being without him.

The ironic thing is that I'm getting nothing out of it. These purchases are supposed to provide convenient, docile pleasure. I don't even dare to touch my boy. I know I should teach him, but the first time I tried, he stirred out of my arms. I am frightened of feeling that pain again, like a wall of water knocking my breath away.

I wait stupidly for a change. Do I expect him to wake me one morning with a kiss and declare his love in a charming accent? I follow him around the apartment. I've begun biting my lips; they're always engorged with blood, ready to kiss. It hurts to be here. But it hurts even more to be away. I am impatient on my way home; I stride at a near run, out of breath. I imagine that he has escaped through the kitchen window — he sits by it for hours, or worse, that when I am gone, he is happy, animated, and smiles.

He doesn't smile. He doesn't cry, either. He looks thoughtful, slightly anxious, afraid, perhaps, that I will pounce on him, though I always hold myself back. I see him now through the doorway, seated at the table, examining my collection of stones. His round, solemn face is in semidarkness; it emerges from the jungle of his incongruously gay curls, I notice his thick lips which look soft like a pale, peeled fruit, his short, plump fingers. He's wearing a wine red sweater I bought him, its high collar hugging his neck. I feel so tender toward that sweater; I want to be where it is now, hands and breasts and arms against his skin, wrapping him, suffocating him with warmth.

Well Julie, please write. How's your garden? I think about July — the tomatoes must be ripe now.

Love,

Carla

The Immune System

Robert P. Kearney

H E CHIDED HIMSELF for dawdling. He had things to do. The truck was missing terribly and had to be looked at, but before he could get to it there were chores in the orchard that would not wait. And more of the tomatoes he kept alongside the shed were bright red and had to be picked immediately. Everything needed him now. But there he sat, scolding himself, with a pain in his lower back. He glared at his coffee. The steam was no longer clouding over it, and the cup was half-empty and cooling between his husky hands.

The phone rang, startling him into action. He scraped the chair back on the kitchen linoleum, leaned over and pulled the receiver off the wall.

"Lo." In the house he felt clumsy. He didn't trust himself. In particular, he didn't trust his hands, which seemed independent and dangerously unpredictable, like Dobermans. So he was very careful with even the receiver, cupping it gently within his palm as he would a live bird.

"Hello, Vernon? This is John Dennison up at the bank. How's everything down at your place?"

"Just fine, Mr. Dennison." He paused, then, out of politeness, asked, "How're things up at the bank?"

"Fine, just fine, thanks."

"Did Marley miss the payment or something, Mr. Dennison?"

"No, Vernon. No problems at all. I was just calling to invite you to come in a little later this afternoon if you can. I think I have a business proposition for you."

"What kind of proposition, Mr. Dennison?"

"Well, it's not the kind of thing we want to discuss over the phone, Vernon. Why don't you just come down. I'd like you to meet a friend of mine and talk a few things over. I think you'll find it interesting."

Vernon considered all his chores for an instant, for as along as he could stretch the word, "wellllll . . ." He had a lot to do, but he recognized that there was a certain protocol involved when dealing with a person to whom you owed a great deal of money and from whom you would surely need to borrow again. "Welll," he said, "sure. You want Marley to come, too? She keeps track of all the books, you know."

"I think this has to do more with your side of the business, Vernon. Does three o'clock sound all right?"

"Fine, Mr. Dennison. See you then." He stood, carefully setting the receiver back in its cradle. For a moment, he stared quietly at the wallpaper. Then he yelled at the ceiling. "Marley?" No answer. He turned and pushed his face close to the screen, yelling into the back yard. "Marley?" At first, there was no answer, then from the shed he could hear her call. There was a thud, and a loud clatter of empty cans. Her head poked through the shed doorway.

Vernon cupped his hands around his mouth. "Are you sure you paid Mr. Dennison this month?"

"Jesus, Vernon, don't I pay him every month? You think you have to tell me everything I'm supposed to do?"

"OK, OK. Just checking." The pain in his back always got worse when she yelled at him. He watched as she turned back to the shed, her thick frame disappearing into the shadows. He turned, and stared back at the black phone.

* * * * * * *

After she'd gone through the garage and the shed and still couldn't find the bottle warmer she'd promised Elaine, she gave up. She made a mental note to go back through the garage and at least *try* to throw away some of the junk. There were mounds of useless, broken appliances out there, and cardboard boxes full of Jack's old clothes. The clothes, she knew, were not exactly useless; Jack used them for working on his car, sometimes wearing them, sometimes using them for rags, sometimes both.

She liked it that he always came back to the house to work on his car. It wasn't the tools, so much, since he had most of what he needed now at his own place. She figured he came mostly because he could always borrow the truck if he needed another part while he had his Chevy in pieces. But she also thought he came because everything in the garage was so familiar and comfortable. The small hydraulic jack was where he had shoved it six months ago, and the box-end wrenches were still loosely arranged at the end of the long plank that served as a work bench. Upstairs, his old room was now filled with sewing and the clothes she was forever intending to iron. But the garage was always very much the same. Once things were deposited there, they were safe for all time. She smiled and suddenly felt guilty for even thinking of throwing away any of it.

Back in the house, she turned on the radio and began to think about dinner. She arched her back, wincing, and decided that dinner could wait until she'd done her exercises.

They were very simple. She had invented them herself. First, she would walk around the living room, trying to shake herself loose. In a slow shimmy, she'd wriggle her arms and shoulders, then her trunk and thighs. This was one reason why she couldn't do her exercises when Vernon was around, why she had to keep an eye on the road. If he'd ever driven up, or walked in, and caught sight of her strutting her bulk around the room, wagging her dappled flesh until it rocked and swung on her bones, he would be disgusted.

She would loosen up, then very slowly bend at the waist. She would never really try to touch her toes. The prospect of it seemed at once wonderful and threatening, like a pregnancy at her age, or winning a million dollars. She would lean forward, pull herself back, then lean forward again. Each time she leaned farther, swooping closer to the floor and the possibility that she might not be able to regain her upright posture. She had never actually been unable to get back, but there were times when it seemed a clear and present danger.

Each time forward she would become more conscious of the gentle pulling and stretching in her lower back. It was marvelous. Jack had teased her, telling her about a ball player who'd solved his back problem by hanging from a bar, first by his hands and then by his knees. This of course was impossible for Marley, but she could imagine how that would also pull the knots out, stretching the muscles like taffy or dough until they were pleasantly flaccid. For her final exercise, she would try to bend forward one vertebra at a time. She imagined she could tell when one of the bone chunks lifted off another, breaking apart like cubes in an ice tray. She would bend as slowly as possible until her body stopped her and then she would come back, one vertebra at a time.

She had never let on about her own techniques, but she'd hinted that Vernon should exercise more. He never listened. He kept on with the liniments and the back rubs she would give him. Sometimes, years before, she'd asked him for backrubs in return, but he was so timid and plodding and unenthusiastic that she quit asking. Once in a while, Vernon took a pain pill. She knew the doctor had prescribed them, and it was not right to judge another particularly in so personal a matter as their health. You could never know, never feel what they felt. But she didn't like him taking pills. On principle, she thought people should take pills only rarely, like a shot. If you took a pill for everything that ails you, she thought, you'd have to keep a small pharmacy up in the bif.

* * * * * * *

He had to slow as the headlights blazed past him. Then he shifted and turned off the main highway and that was when the truck died. It made no noise, just simply lost steam and the steering wheel went heavy and unresponsive in his thick hands. Vernon swore loudly. There was a good slant downhill and he tried to pop the clutch a couple of times, but the engine only gagged and spit and never properly turned over. Finally, the hulk coasted to a stop at the bottom of the incline and Vernon got out. He slammed the door, and immediately felt foolish for making such a show of anger. After a moment he climbed back into the cab and turned the key, but had no expectations that the truck would start. Its failure, in fact, seemed perfectly logical. Without it, his life would have seemed just a bit brighter and wealthier, as a result of Mr. Thatcher. Now, true to form, the world was undercutting all his gains. He gathered up the literature Thatcher had given him and struck off down the dirt road.

Once, Vernon had believed in progress. In getting ahead. Now he was convinced that there was only movement, toiling like a silkworm, spinning a cocoon that was never finished. Working like hell for a transformation that was stolen for someone else's suit or pajamas, their transformation.

As he walked up to the house, he could see that the lights were off except in the den, where she would be watching the "Tonight Show" and paging through a magazine. He reached the house as the light went out and another came on over the stairway. He scraped his shoes and went in.

"Vernon?" she asked from the top of the stairs.

"Yes, dear."

"I didn't hear the truck."

He looked up the stairs at her. "Yes. There's a reason why you didn't. The old heap decided to call it quits down at the bottom of the hill. I'll have to go look at it tomorrow."

She sighed and said, "Oh, no," and then went into the bathroom. He began to mount the stairs, but remembered the literature he still held, and went back down.

Later, after she had finished in the bathroom and he had finished and they were both in bed, she asked him what had happened.

"I don't know. I just pulled off the road and it killed."

"No, I mean about Mr. Dennison."

Oh, Mr. Dennison's friend Thatcher wants to buy our crop. The whole crop. Everything."

"Is he a canner?"

"No. Not exactly."

"Then what's he want with an orchard's worth of apricots."

"The pits. He's gonna sell the fruit, he figures, but what he's really interested in is the pits. He's thinking about making Laetrile."

"Really. Isn't that interesting." There was a long pause, and she said, "I didn't know people could just do that. Just make it like that."

"Well, I don't know that they can. I have a feeling that it's sort of illegal." He turned to her, although they could not see each other in the dark. "He said he'd buy all the crop and pay ten percent over market. But we couldn't tell anyone who we sold it to. Mum."

"Didn't you think to ask him if it was illegal?"

"Thought of it, but decided not to. Figured I might not like the answer." He laughed. "I figured it wasn't illegal for me. I'm just selling fruit." He laughed again, then asked her, "Does that stuff work or what?"

"I don't know, really. There've been so many articles I just haven't been able to keep up."

"Thatcher gave me some literature about it. Let's both go over it and see what we think."

"O.K." He thought her voice sounded happy, cheered by the

prospect of a new field of research and a new decision to be made. She liked to work, and she made the work easier for him. He reached out and stroked her head awkwardly in the dark, and she moved toward him on the pillow. They kissed once, gently, and rolled away from each other, their rears touching, their bodies crouched under the dust-colored quilt, looking from above like an enormous moth.

* * * * * * *

Early, while the sun was still trying to put shade and density in a cloudless sky, Marley came down into the kitchen. Her motions were automatic. She reached into the refrigerator, pulling out a grapefruit, which she held on the cutting board. She sliced through it quickly, and left only a tiny dribble of juice.

A scallop of thin, shiny pamphlets lay on the table. She picked up the first and read the title—"Cancer's Seven Warning Signs." Holding it, she shuffled through the others. Laetrile. Cancer. One was titled, "How People Die in America," and she wondered if they mentioned housework. Cancer again.

She stacked the pamphlets, thinking she would look through them later, while Vernon was out. She fed gas to the burner under the kettle but it wouldn't light until she removed the kettle and waved over the apertures, forcing the gas back into the pilot light. Flame whooshed out at her passing hand.

She knew the pamphlets would say it worked. They would have to say that. The pamphlets would say it worked but the articles and doctors would say it didn't. No one would say if it was right to give it to people even if it didn't work. The pamphlets would surely never mention it, because they said it worked. And the articles and the doctors were busy making their points and wouldn't grudge a point in favor of the stuff. To Marley, giving a dying man anything he could use smacked of Christian conduct. On the other hand, selling him snake oil could hardly be called charity.

Bubbles were forming on the bottom of the skillet. There was no reckoning what Vernon might do. He might sell and keep quiet, or he might sell and talk, or he might not sell at all, on ethical grounds. He was a hard one to figure. Sometimes she would catch herself staring at him with the same disorientation that she felt when she opened the wrong dryer at the laundromat, and reached her hands in among the warm and alien clothes.

She opened the refrigerator again and pulled out the eggs. She cracked one on the edge of the pan and let it slide into the boiling water. Upstairs, he was flushing the toilet, thumping around between the bathroom and the bedroom, soon to come down. Even if he were acting on ethical grounds, she thought, there was no predicting which ethical grounds he would act on. Sometimes he earnestly tried to imitate Christ, and those times he was a marvel of patience and generosity. Other times he was imitating his father, or a former boss, or John Wayne. She thought these were all very noble men but difficult to reconcile in one Vernon.

Suddenly, she decided that she did not want to read the pamphlets. There seemed no sense to studying something terrible that you couldn't understand, couldn't judge, couldn't do anything about. She swept up the slick, folded papers, carried them into the living room, and set them neatly in a corner of the bookcase. Later, that evening, she could watch television or read and he could sit under the pole lamp in the living room and go through the pamphlets. It would be all right then, but it was not breakfast reading.

* * * * * * *

Vernon read through them without paying a lot of attention. He'd been sure from the beginning that the stuff didn't work, and was only paging through the pamphlets because he'd said he would. He also had a certain curiousity about the disease. But he knew the stuff didn't work, had known it as soon as he saw Thatcher and shook hands with him. Some shake from the hip, the palm broad and firm. Some from the shoulder, the reach long, the hand like an arrowhead. But Thatcher had been fussy and too high, the palm toward himself. That was enough to know about Thatcher and his business. Vernon's judgment in this case was as immediate and as irrevocable as murder, and he derived a certain satisfaction from this.

He went into the other room and sat down. Marley smiled at him, but said nothing until the commercial.

"Well, what do you think?"

He laughed. "Load'a bunk."

She frowned and thought a minute, her eyes still following the images on the screen. "Well?"

"Well, we could sell, It's not like we have to be responsible for everything everyone does to our fruit. On the other hand, maybe you shouldn't sell corn to a moonshiner, or bullets to a killer." He rubbed his forehead with the heal of his hand, grimacing without real cause. "I don't know. I don't think it'll make you blind or kill you."

"No." Marley pulled one slippered foot up, and hugged it to her thigh. "But I think some people take it instead of what they ought to. I think. I should dig out those articles."

"Yes," Vernon said. "Do that." For an instant something else crossed his mind, but then the commercials were over and Johnny Carson was back, and Vernon's attention was diverted.

* * * * * * *

Even before she'd dug out the articles she suspected he would sell to Thatcher. The money was good enough and the ethics sufficiently muddled to accomodate almost any decision. Nevertheless, she spent two hours rummaging through stacks of musty old magazines and newspapers, and could only find one article, which confirmed that people often took the stuff instead of prescribed drugs or x-rays or going under the knife. She considered this for a moment and decided that it was very understandable. She tried to weigh the odds of one treatment against the bleak chances of the other, while adding in all the different varieties of pain and their duration, and then she remembered another stack of magazines that she had found while looking for the bottle-warmer.

She went quietly across the back yard, turned into the shed and screamed. Vernon, hanging by his knees from a roof beam, screamed back and nearly fell on his head. She saw his legs jerk and threw herself toward him in a confused attempt at rescue, but he swatted her back with upsidedown arms.

"Jesus Christ, woman, you don't have the . . ." The rest of the torrent was lost in a series of grunts as he pulled himself up to the crossbeam, released his legs, and lowered himself to the top of the work bench.

He climbed down shaking, his face scarlet with what she imagined was a mix of exertion, anger, embarrassment, and gravity.

She began, "Vernon, I'm sorry, I'm . . . I just . . ." but he cut her off.

"Not one word. Not one." He stalked past her, into the yard, and stopped and turned around. He was still angry and his arms were pumping up and down. The scolding he wanted to give her didn't come, and this added to his embarrassment. He raged silently, the furor steeping until his eyes bugged out. That was when she got the giggles. She looked away but he saw her and it pushed his anger to its peak. Then it disappeared. He relaxed, went slack. "It's just my damn back, Marley. It's killing me sometimes, and I just thought I'd try anything . . ."

She was still giggling and trying to suppress it, feeling very girlish in the effort. She approached and stood beside him, hugging him with both arms. But still unable to look up at him without giggling. He put an arm around her and was silent, and she suddenly felt guilty. She said, "Can I show you something?" She led him toward the house, saying, "If you promise not to tease, I'll show you what ! do."

In the living room, she explained the first step. "You just kind.. walk around and let everything relax. Like . . ." and she tried to do her loosening exercises but found that she was too tense with him there All her muscles held firm and formal. "This isn't working," she said. She stopped, took a deep breath, and tried again. This time was better.

"I can't do that," Vernon said. "You look like a complete moron."

"Just try it. You didn't look exactly bright hanging from your monkey bar in the shed, you know."

He scowled and walked woodenly around the room.

"No. No. More like this," she said, heaving herself up and then relaxing.

His next turn around the room was less stolid, and she encouraged him to throw a bit more shake into it. "Kinda shimmy a little."

"Oh, shit."

"Come on, just try it." She stepped back and watched her husband of twenty-five years flounce back and forth in their living room and she got the giggles again. Vernon didn't stop. Chortling himself, his head wagging and his face aglow with silliness, he said, "It's not helping any and I feel like a damn fairy." Then they heard the squeal of springs and the radio as a car turned in.

"Oh, Jesus, it's Jack," she said, and they both yelped and dashed into the kitchen and quickly sat down at the table where their son found them, seconds later, flushed and goofy-eyed with wild smiles twitching in and out of their faces.

* * * * * * *

The next morning, Vernon discovered he had cancer.

He was driving home in the desperate pick-up, after meeting with Thatcher, and he was figuring his odds. It was an absent calculation, more with weights an vectors than with numbers. There had been years working as a roofer, breathing asbestos from shingles, and then there were all the chemicals he'd handled growing things. And of course there was smoking, which he'd finally kicked, but only after twenty years. The odds were already very much in favor of having cancer, and that did not include all the deadly substances that had not even been recognized yet.

He was aware of a thousand petty discomforts, in his hands and his feet, in the calf that pulled to push the foot on the acclerator. Suddenly, he became aware of a swelling in his crotch, a fullness that spread down into his scrotum and up, into his intestines. He drove farther, still analyzing, still taking stock, and the sense of swelling subsided. Then his back erupted in pain, and for a moment the pain reached into his bowels to just the spot where the swelling had reached up. He shuddered and knew. Knew as clearly as he knew anything. The word had been tossed casually between them all morning; now it returned and rooted. There was no denying it, no revocation of knowledge. His chest was full of his heart and he couldn't breathe correctly. He pulled over and cursed.

* * * * * * *

After the movie had ended and she'd turned off the lamp, she went back into the living room. Vernon was still there, sitting in roughly the same position, wearing the same expression of apathetic surprise. She had tried sympathy and she had tried straightforward worry and nothing worked. Now she let contempt veil her continued concern.

"Sure you don't want a beer or something?"

"Nope. Thanks. I'll be up in a minute."

He lied the same way every night, except when he fell asleep in the chair. Then she could wake him and lead the way to bed, and he'd be too loggy to resist.

She went up, prepared herself, and climbed into bed. The same day that Vernon had declared his diagnosis, they'd driven back to town together. She was scared. Dr. Green listened and then examined Vernon. While she was by herself the fear got worse, got deep and inflated. Then Vernon came out, and they waited together. This was pure and unnerving waiting, unadulterated by reading or errands or any but the smallest talk. Time became elongated, stretched around them. Finally, Vernon had drawn himself up and said, "It doesn't matter, what he says. I'm gonna die anyways." She admired this bravery and it brought the tears much closer. Then Vernon added that whatever the results showed, he knew he had cancer and would die of it and it was only a matter of time. Her sorrow gave way to confusion, which was suppressed. She permitted herself to doubt that she had heard him correctly, or, if she had, to have somehow misunderstood his bravery.

Eventually, Dr. Green appeared and told them that there was nothing wrong with Vernon other than an occasionally overactive imagination and his back, which had been bunged-up for some time and would undoubtedly remain so. Marley watched the doctor closely as he spoke and was relatively confident that he was telling the truth, and found that a comforting reinforcement to such happy news.

Vernon only nodded and thanked the doctor. She thought he was acting then, still being brave. She followed his looks and his words closely, as closely as she had followed Dr. Green's, looking for subterranean jubilance, for some sign of undirected gratitude or praise. She waited patiently for several days but he only became more indifferent, more detached, and this irritated her. By rights he should have danced around the room and hugged her and the doctor and then they should have gone home and planned a vacation. Jack and Joan had gone to the Bahamas for their honeymoon and the pictures were so pretty. She had only seen the ocean at New York and San Francisco, and it was not at all like the water in Jack's pictures, which was clear and turquoise and which, Jack said, has phosphorus in it so that it glowed when stirred up at night.

None of this had interested Vernon much before and certainly did not enter his mind now. He'd turned morbid. It made her distraught—almost as distraught as if he really had had cancer.

She threw back the covers and went downstairs. He said nothing to her. She pulled the ottoman over and sat directly in front of him.

"You're not going to die, Vernon."

"We're all gonna die, Marley." He gave her an uneven smile.

"Come off it," she said. "You don't believe that."

"It's got nothing to do with belief. I know it."

"Just like you knew you had cancer?" She sneered, putting it on as thick as she could without being comical, but he wouldn't be angered. "Listen," she continued, "if death is just around the corner, let's enjoy what life we have left. Let's go over to the Eagle, or to a movie. Cripes, let's go to Paris or India or Tahiti. Why not?"

Vernon shook his head. "Let's just take some of those pain pills and go to bed." He rose and shook the wrinkles out of his pants. He waited.

She said, "You're lying to me. I'm going to go up and you're going to stay here."

"I'll go up," he said.

"Then you'll come back later."

"No, I won't."

She got up slowly, her eyes on his. He went up the stairs ahead of her and turned into the bathroom. She crawled into bed and waited. He always said he was coming to bed and never did, but she waited for him nevertheless. She wished she could close her eyes and know he would soon be beside her, or know that he would quietly shuffle downstairs again. Either would be better than staring wide-eyed at the ceiling and waiting. She was sorry now that she had asked him to come upstairs. If she hadn't forced him into this, she would know what to expect. Suddenly she rolled over and covered her head with a pillow and hummed softly to herself but still couldn't help hearing.

* * * * * * *

Vernon let him buy the first one. He knew that Jack felt awkward about this—about the forced proximity, the weight, the sheer tonnage of respect and firmness and gentleness that his son was attempting to juggle. Letting the boy buy the first one put him in a strong spot. Vernon would have preferred to skip the scene altogether, but that was impossible. Jack was resolved. He felt he had to do something and was going to do it, because that was the way Vernon had raised him.

"Look, Dad. You've got a bad back. And that's . . . well, it's a shame. it's a bitch. But it isn't the end of the goddamn world."

"That's not the point."

"Well, what *is* the point? You've been so . . . so down lately. It's worrying everyone. Mom's about out of her nut."

Vernon said, "I just meant that the back wasn't anything special. It's been bad for years." He paused, trying to decide how much he should say. He didn't want to say anything that could be interpreted as raving, because that would only frighten everyone more. He could not tell him that he knew he had cancer, even if Dr. Green didn't. Dr. Green would know soon enough, after the single, monstrous cell— humped and club-footed—had tried to escape and instead only made another. And then both made another, and the whole colony advanced exponentially within his body. But he couldn't say that to his son.

Instead he said, "I don't know what it is," and he smiled apologetically.

"But you're just so damn spooky, Dad. If you'd just sleep in a bed a couple nights a week."

He was getting sarcastic now, but Vernon let it pass. He wished he could come right out and tell him. He reconsidered, then dropped the idea. If he didn't know he had cancer, he couldn't understand. He could be told, but he would never understand that there are things you have to do. You cannot dawdle in bars, you cannot waste your time sleeping. Jack still believed, under it all, that he would never die. He was like a man who has so much money that he doesn't believe he can ever spend it all. Then, when he gets to the last dollar, he becomes filled with the worst sort of self-hatred, the worst remorse and contempt, thinking, "If only I'd invested a little. If only I'd bought this instead of that." And it was in that destitute, impoverished condition that most people kicked off. Vernon, on the other hand, had figured it out while he still had ten dollars left. He never thought he could regain his millions, but he wanted to spend the ten dollars wisely. He wanted, more than anything, the vision of the pauper while he still had a pittance. He was determined to understand fully. He would do his best to struggle in private, like hanging from his knees, but he really didn't care who was watching. He was beyond embarrassment.

Jack was saying, "What's happened is you've gotten just a little overwrought. That's all. You've let this one thing get under your skin, and now its grown all out of proportion. All you need now is to just relax, get away from it. Have a few beers now and then."

Vernon thought, Chemo-therapy.

"Go to the movies. Watch TV."

And your radiation. Then he thought, But I don't think we can cut. Maybe Thatcher and I could sit down and discuss the Bible. But he said, "OK. Sure. I'll give it a try."

Jack's brow lowered, and he took a long, shallow draught of air. "That's the spirit." He rapped his knuckles on the bar top for emphasis. "Now, you buy the next one," he added humorously.

* * * * * * *

The static over the phone was high and irregular, like animal noises.

"Hello, Marley? This is Mr. Dennison. Can you hear me?"

"Sure."

"Good. How are things?"

'Oh, fine. We're all going to hell in a lunchbucket up here. How's the bank?"

"Excuse me?"

"Nevermind, Mr. Dennison. What can I do for you?"

"I was just calling because Vernon was supposed to meet with Mr. Thatcher and me today, and he hasn't shown up. What time did he leave?"

"He's having some problems today, Mr. Dennison. Bad case of back trouble extending right up through his entire brains, I think. Listen," she sighed now, realizing that it was falling on her shoulders to finish the deal and make sure the harvesters were contracted and someone had trucks ready and without Vernon it would all cost more and that would nearly wipe out all the advantage they were to have had from dealing with Thatcher. "Listen," she repeated, "I'll come in myself. You figure Mr. Thatcher can hang around another half hour? Thank you. See you shortly."

* * * * * * *

Vernon discovered that he already knew part of the secret. Everyone knew it but denied it, smuggled it with them in a hollow brain lobe, a hollow chamber in the heart. But he was no bootlegger; he freely acknowledged that death was constant, continuous, never-ending.

He went out into the pasture, killing things and noting his indifference. He moved at a fair clip, treading out the life in grass, weeds, ants and spiders and more grass. And into the patch of mint down by the creek. The old and young and embryonic, the male and female and hermaphroditic. Natural events in the billions were upended. Inanimate objects, seeking their destinies, were frustrated.

As before, he stopped at the edge of the quarry and noted the wreckage below. Parts of cars and farm equipment and other, nameless scraps of metal littered the bottom, dull and rusty, with an occasional glint of chrome.

He went to the quarry to scare himself. He would stand at the edge and lean forward. He thought that by confronting himself with great danger, with impending death, he might prematurely learn the secrets of a natural deathbed. He was trying to simulate that moment just prior to elimination, to bankruptcy. Unfortunately, he found that he couldn't hoodwink himself. He leaned over the edge and waited, the moment of death theoretically closer, theoretically veering in on him at dizzying speed, but no truth was revealed. He suspected himself of false hope, of doubting the obvious and inescapable fact of his demise. He wavered faintly, measuring danger in fractions, in matrices of impulse and degrees and inches. He waited. Finally, nothing happened, and not wishing everything to be resolved by his inate clumsiness, he straightened, turned and returned along the path of his carnage, thinking that there was so much more to be figured, the task increasingly complex and deviling.

* * * * * * *

Marley first put the magazine down on the nightstand and then set the shot glass on top, not caring that it would leave a small glistening, rippling ring on Secretary James E. Schlesinger's forehead. She looked at both the magazine and the whiskey and realized that they were actually additional obstacles between her and her sweet sleep. But she resolved to finish at least the whiskey, because she had promised it to herself earlier in the day, in the orchard, and it seemed like a promise that should be consumated, like certain awkward and unwanted courtesies.

She sat on the bed and then flopped back, her weight and exhaustion seeming to burn her form into the mattress. She was numb with work, except in her back, which was a solid slab of taut muscle, as rigid as if the vertebrae had been welded together. She thought of the whiskey but could not find the wherewithal to reach for it.

It's finished, she thought, meaning the orchard although immediately the thought took on a life of its own and began to blanket many things, some of which were only vague in her mind. This frightened her just enough to cause her to sit up and reach for the shot glass.

She sipped a little, her tongue splashing the liquor behind her teeth. She had not even seen any money. It'd gone directly into the bank with part going toward the loan and part into savings and just a bit into checking. Mr. Dennison had been very nice and reminded her of the original agreement not to reveal the deal with Mr. Thatcher and the bank. That was when Marley realized that Thatcher and Dennison were partners. She wondered if Vernon had thought of it, but decided quickly that it didn't matter.

Vernon is a lost soul, she thought, and even though she rebuked herself for it immediately afterward she knew it was not a judgment, only a statement of fact. She still loved him and was not sure but that he might be a lot smarter than the rest of them in some ways. But she was fed up with him. He had become too overwhelmed with one thing, too concentrated. It was not that his thinking was not important but it was wrong to be so concentrated, to lose all awareness of her and the orchard and Jack just because he'd thought he'd had cancer when it was only his back. She knew that Thatcher had set him off but didn't blame him. She figured that if that was the way Vernon was, that was the way he was and it would've happened sooner or later.

In her mind she had already sold the house and farm many times and put Vernon in an institution. She would review scenes from the fantasy often, hoping that she would be ready for the inevitable. She sighed, thinking that Vernon was perhaps brilliantly right, was a genius, but would still have to be locked away. He was not dangerous, but he would have to be looked in on once in a while by someone who was competent to handle this sort of thing. This brilliance that had dulled so much of the rest of him.

And for herself, there would be a long vacation, to the Bahamas or any other place where turquoise water stretched out to the horizons. She would find a masseur, a nice retired masseur, with hands as big and solid as a spade but tender as a seed. And they would travel. There would be no sex, only railroad cars with glass domes and airplanes and cruise ships.

She threw down the rest of the whiskey and slid under the covers. She was in the habit of leaving the hall light on and the door ajar in case Vernon wandered up in the night. When she turned out the lamp, a plane of light bisected the bed. In the hall she could see a fragment of the bannister and the dull sheen of the hardwood floor.

She had never seen phosphorescent water. She could not imagine it was very bright, but surely it was not a pallid, trumped-up wonder like the caves or reptile farms along some highways. It would be marvelously and softly lustrous, perhaps with little sparkles, bright points of light shining in the wake of the boat as the band played and the sure hands of the masseur, who was retired but not yet bald, led her across the dance floor. She would dance and drink and dance more, until something actually came up and forced her to stop, until something killed her, until her lymph nodes were as hard and swollen as a Caribbean grapefruit or until she was so lithe and slender, so svelte and limber. that she could touch her toes.

Contributor's Notes

R Bartkowech has taught creative writing for 2 years at the University of Colorado. His poetry, fiction, and reviews have appeared in *The Little Magazine, MidAtlantic Review, Oyez Review, Mississippi Review*, etc. He has completed several volumes of writing including *Multiple Abrasions* (poems), *Contagion* (short stories), and *Aspiration to Plato's Olympus* (a novel). He is co-founder of Barking Dog Press.

Regina de Cormier-Shekerjian has published poetry and fiction in *The Smith, Porch, Willow Springs, Wind, Assembling*, and a recently published book received the National Jewish Book Award. Her visual poetry has been exhibited at Pratt Institute of Art, the Los Angeles Institute of Contemporary Art and at various universities. She lives in New Platz, New York.

Patricia Weaver Francisco is a fiction and freelance writer. Originally from Michigan, she now lives in Minneapolis, Minnesota. She was awarded a Minnesota State Arts Board grant for fiction and has been published in *Great River Review*. Currently she is completing the novel from which the piece in this anthology is exerpted.

Kate Green received her M.A. from Boston University where she studied writing with Anne Sexton and John Cheever. Her book of poems, *The Bell In The Silent Body* is available from Minnesota Writers' Publishing House (1977). She works with the Minnesota Writers In The Schools Program and is presently at work on a novel.

Robert P. Kearney was born and raised in Richfield, Minnesota. He attended De La Salle High School and Dartmouth College. He now lives in south Minneapolis. For the past two years, he has worked as a mid-level bureaucrat and occasional teacher. His work has appeared in literary journals, magazines and newspapers.

Terry Kennedy has work published in *Chelsea, Primavera, Shameless Hussy Review, Bachy*, and *Green's Magazine*. She does investigative reporting and is at work on her first novel. Her second book of poems is forthcoming from Second Coming Press (San Francisco).

Lynn Lauber grew up in a "mean little industrial town" in northwest Ohio. She later attended the creative writing program at Ohio State University. Since moving to Rockland County, New York, she has been involved in a number of women's writing workshops. Her work has appeared in the *Ohio Journal* and *Dialogue* and she is at work on a collection of short stories.

Mary Logue is a native Minnesotan who makes her living as a writer. She works in the Minnesota Writers In The Schools Program and freelances as a music reviewer and editor. She recently finished editing *Thief of Sadness*, PLS Press, a book of poetry by mentally retarded women. She is currently working on a screenplay, a poetry manuscript and a novel.

William Meissner teaches creative writing at St. Cloud State University. Nine of his short stories have been published in several literary journals including *Center, Gallimaufry, Perspectives, Great River Review, The Unicorn,* and *North Country*. He has been awarded a Creative Writing Fellowship from the National Endowment for the Arts. His first book of poetry, *Learning to Breathe Underwater*, was published recently by Ohio University Press (Athens, Ohio). He is presently completing a collection of short stories entitled *Waiting For The Family Rain*.

Warren Schmidt was born in 1942, lives in Minneapolis, and is one of four people in the United States who approved of our military involvement in Viet Nam.

Judith Serin was born in New Jersey. She has a B.A. from Bennington College, where she studied with poet Michael Dennis Browne, and an M.A. in Creative Writing from San Francisco State University. Over fifty of her poems have appeared in magazines and anthologies, including *New Poets: Women* (Les Femmes, 1976), *Contemporary Women Poets* (Merlin Press, 1977), *Dear Gentlepersons: A Collection of Bay Area Women Poets* (Hartmus Press, 1978), *Laurel Review, The Ohio Journal,* and *Bachy*. Her short stories have appeared in *Love Stories by New Women* (Red Clay Books, 1978) and *Great Sky Review*. She currently lives in Berkeley, California where she teaches adult education creative writing classes.

Lawrence Sutin has had stories and reviews published in *Writers Introduce Writers, 25 Minnesota Writers* (Nodin Press), and *Minnesota Monthly*. Like every other sentient being in the universe, he is working on a novel.

Thomas Zigal was raised in Texas City, on the Texas Gulf Coast. He has an M.A. in Creative Writing from Stanford University. He currently works as an editor for an educational publishing company in Austin, Texas. His short fiction has appeared in *New Letters*, *Texas Quarterly*, *The Pawn Review*, *The Bicentennial Collection of Texas Short Stories*, etc. Thorp Springs Press will publish his first novel, *Playland*.

Mary Cheney Library
586 Main Street
Manchester, CT